MW01282801

ONE TIMER

AN NASHVILLE ASSASSINS NOVEL

TONI ALEO

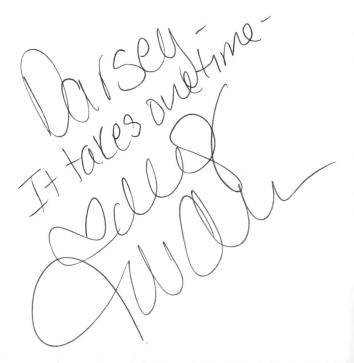

Darsey —
It takes one time —

Copyright © 2019 by Toni Aleo

All rights reserved.

One Timer is a work of fiction. No part of this book may be reproduced in any form or by any electronic or mechanical means, including information storage and retrieval systems, without written permission from the author, except for the use of brief quotations in a book review.

Editing by: Lisa Hollett of Silently Correcting Your Grammar

Proofing by: Jenny Rarden

Cover Design: Lori Jackson Design

❀ Created with Vellum

This book is for someone I consider to be very special—Janet.
Janet was full of such beautiful life. She was a hopeless romantic and
funny as all get-out.
She was the first person to read Taking Shots, chapter by chapter. I
wrote it in her basement when I wasn't at work. She was one of my
first supporters. I lost her on 9/15/2019, and my heart aches at the
loss.
Love you, Janet.

Janet Leigh Moore
2/1/83 – 9/15/2019

HEY, HOW YOU DOIN'?

Why don't you join my newsletter for updates on new releases, sales, deleted scenes, and more? Sign up with confidence. NO SPAM EVER! JOIN NOW!

SHE'S GONNA BE THE DEATH OF ME, JAKOB!

JAKOB

I feel all children should just accept their parents are always right.

We've been there. We made the bad decisions. We slept with people we shouldn't have. We drank until we were drunker than a skunk. We jumped out of cars and fought with exes outside Taco Bell. We worked hard and then hardly worked, which resulted in ramen for a week. We were broke, we struggled, and then we realized that our parents were always right. I know this, I learned it the hard way, and I ignored all my parents' wishes. They didn't want me to chase my dreams of the National Hockey League. They wanted me to work for the family, and while I ignored them and it worked out great for me, I know that will not be the case for my baby.

So, if she could just realize it before she ruins her life, that would be great.

Instead, I sit in the middle of the living room as my daughter screams at my wife. Journey, my son, who is mighty smart, sits beside me with his headphones on as he kills zombies on the Xbox. I wish I could join, but my wife would probably cut me in half. But neither of the women in my family is listening to me.

"Mom! You don't understand! I love him. Like, with my whole soul! And he loves me the same!"

Of course he does. Our daughter, Allison, is the perfect combination of her mother and me. She's built like Harper, tall and slim. She's got muscles from years of volleyball and my dark green eyes that, in the right light, sparkle from the flecks of gold. Her hair is a light brown that falls down her back like a mane. Harper always keeps her own hair shorter and her eyes are blue, but when they stand beside each other, they look like twins. Problem is, my daughter has her mother's mouth, which is why it's never quiet around here. They've been going at it since Allison was twelve, and sometimes, I wish she were more like me. Let the water roll off her back. But for some reason, she is always geared up to fight. Or maybe that's Harper; she brings it out in our girl. For me, Harper brings all the good feelings out of me.

Even after all these years, my wife still knocks me on my ass with her beauty. She keeps me on my toes, keeps me laughing, and she's one hell of a mother. Journey is easy; he plays video games when he's not on the ice. But when he's on it, she's in the stands screaming his name. She is the best at homework, which is fantastic since I struggle with the English written word. Even after living in the States most of my adult life, I still struggle. Harper doesn't care. She does it all. There isn't a game of Allison's she's missed. She has been team mom for the last five years. How she is team mom for the college team is beyond me, but I'm so proud. Allison needs her mom.

They may fight, but they love each other more than anything. Which is why this fight is killing me. I want to blame the guy—Taco. Yes, this dumbass goes by the name of

Taco, sometimes Doritos Locos Taco if he's feeling spicy. *Insert the eye roll.* And truth be told, I hate him. I let my hatred for him slide most of the time because of how much Allison loves him. First-time adult love is rough. I remember mine; I married her. So, yeah. I get it. The guy has no choice but to notice my princess. She's her mom made over, but he doesn't get to take her away from everything and ruin her life.

I know I sound dramatic, but Allison is on a full ride to Bellevue. Not just for volleyball but for academics too. She's not only talented on the court, but she's a damn genius! Again, taking from both of us. My athletics and her momma's smarts. She took a year off after high school to play volleyball in Brazil. She already had the scholarship lined up, but she wanted to improve her skills even more before she started on their team.

While I understand she's gotta make decisions on her own, fall on her face and all that jazz, can't she do that when she's done with school? She's worked so damn hard. Which is what Harper is trying to tell her.

"Ally, I get it. Baby, I do. I promise I do. But you have a full ride, sweetheart. A full ride. You can't give that up to run off to Texas. What the hell is in Texas? Will you go to school? Will you play? I mean, you're the team's setter. They need you!"

"Princess, Mom is right. It's not only yourself you'll be hurting—it'll be your team."

"But I love him!" she screams, and then the tears start. "He's leaving for work, and he won't do long-distance. I can't lose him."

"Why?" I ask, and apparently, that is the wrong question.

"Daddy! I love him," she says, her eyes wide and flooded with tears. I hate when she cries. "He is my best friend, my other half."

Was I this dumb? I might have been. Harper tried to get rid of me over and over again, but I wasn't going anywhere.

"But Ally, darling, if it is the same for him, why can't he do long-distance? No man should ask you to give it all up for him. Daddy never asked that of me."

I nod, though neither of them is looking at me. I have been prone to injuries my whole career—and each time, Harper was there. I wouldn't let her miss work or anything with the kids for my sake. Somehow, she made it work. I think when I retired, Harper was sadder than me. She loved watching me play, watching me live my dreams. But what she didn't realize was she is my dreams. She stood beside me on the ice with our children as we watched my jersey rise to the rafters. It hangs with my buddies' up there—Shea Adler, Alex Welch, and Lucas Brooks. It's pretty damn awesome, especially since I'm on the special teams coaching staff for the Nashville Assassins as their lead coach. Elli Adler may have had to let me retire, but she wouldn't let me coach anywhere but for her. We won the Cup last season, and we want it again this year. Things are going well. The start of the season has been somewhat successful. Our power play is junk, but we'll get there. If Allison leaves, I'm worried my focus will be shaken.

I can't lose my baby yet. Not to some dude named Taco. What will they name their kids? Chalupa and Burrito? Fuck no. Don't get me wrong—the guy is nice, but he isn't what she needs. It was fine as some fleeting romance. She met him at a party on campus. He doesn't go to Bellevue—or anywhere, for that matter.

Higher education is a waste of time and money, bro. It's The Man. He's making us do it all. We're wasting our lives for money when we need the experience!

His words, not mine. I'm all for the experiences and I live my life to the fullest, but how am I supposed to do anything if I don't have money? I grew up dirt poor. I mean, really poor. The only experience I had growing up was watching my neighbor snort coke off one of his whore's ass cheeks. Now, I am experiencing watching my kids live their dreams, while loving the best woman I know. I need money for that. Maybe it is *The Man*, but I don't care. I work for what I want, and that kid—he doesn't work. The reason he is moving to Texas is because his grandma is giving him a house and a car if he comes to live with her. So, he wants my daughter, who is doing fantastic here, the starting setter for the Bellevue Bullies and with three years of a 4.0, to give all that up to follow him. When she has half a year left?

You know what? I hate the guy even more.

"You're not thinking clearly. What will you do when you get there?"

Allison looks away, a tell that she has no damn clue. "I don't know. We haven't gotten that far. We'll live with his grandma, and I'll find work."

"Find work…" my wife says slowly, her eyes burning with anger. "Your work is getting a damn education so you can make a life for yourself."

"But Mom, I don't want to work to make a living. I want to live."

For the love of God. I let my head fall. "Allison, my love, you can do both. Your life is what you make it. I had nothing. Now I have everything because I worked for it."

She throws her arms in the air. "But my life will be shit without him."

Journey snorts beside me. "Yeah, because your life is so great with him. You spend more time making sure he isn't cheating on you than you do enjoying him."

Harper gasps. I look at the side of my amazing boy's face, and I nod. The kid doesn't say much and I may have forgotten he was in the room, but damn if he didn't just drop a bomb.

"He cheated? On you? He's lucky you're even allowing him to breathe your air!"

Allison rolls her eyes. And yeah, Harper may have been a

bit dramatic there. "God, shut up, Jour! You don't even know him."

"Because he's an asshole," he says.

"Journey! Your mouth!"

He shrugs. "I'm just saying what everyone is thinking."

He sure is, but Allison doesn't like that. She throws her hands up and yells, "No one is thinking that! He is wonderful!"

Before Journey can say more, I press my hand to his knee. "Allison, it has nothing to do with him and everything to do with you. We want the best for you. This is not the best. I mean, look at Shea's niece. She threw away everything—"

"And now she is happily married with babies."

By the look Harper gives me, I realize maybe that wasn't the best example. "But she suffered first."

"Taco loves me. He wouldn't hurt me."

"Anyone named Taco isn't someone I would trust," Journey says simply. But before Allison can snap at him, Harper holds up her palms.

"Okay, we can't change your mind on him, and that's fine. But here is the deal, Allison. We won't be there when he drops your ass like we all know he will. If you're willing to throw away everything you worked for, all the money we put into volleyball for you, the hours we spent doing math with you, then I'm sorry, you will leave this house as naked as you were the day we brought you here."

Allison's eyes widen. "What?"

"You heard me," Harper says sternly, but I see the hurt in her eyes. She doesn't want to do this to our girl. "We will cancel your bank card, we will take the car, and everything will stay here. So, think long and hard if you want to give up all that—along with your college career."

And with that, Harper walks out of the room. When she reaches the hall, though, I can still see her, and she drops her shoulders. Fuck, I think I hate it more when Harper cries.

"She's not serious!" Allison hollers at me, but I don't have to answer her.

Journey does. "Of course she is. They've given us everything, and you want to throw away the one thing you've been working for since you were ten for some guy? For a genius who wants to be a dentist, you're a real idiot."

That obviously offends my daughter. Offends me a bit too, but he isn't wrong. "Like you even understand. Girls aren't even on your radar! Or guys, for that matter."

She stomps away, eventually slamming her door as I look down at Journey, who doesn't seem to give two shits about what his sister just said. I didn't think he would, though. He really just goes with the flow. He's our easy kid, the one who doesn't cause a fuss. He does him, and I love that about him. However, I've always wondered if he was gay. He's never given any indication or behaved stereotypically in any way, but I've also never seen him with a girlfriend. Then again, I've never seen him with a boyfriend either.

When his eyes meet mine, I raise a brow. "Got something to tell me?"

He shakes his head. "Your daughter is an idiot?"

I want to laugh, but I don't. I don't want this to be a laughing matter. "I mean about what she said."

He looks away, swallowing hard. "Nope."

I nod and tap his knee before I get up. "Good talk."

"Always."

A smile pulls at my lips as I head toward our bedroom. It doesn't matter if Journey is or isn't. I love the dude, and he'll always be my best friend. When I reach our room, I push open the door to find Harper on the phone.

"Elli, I don't get it. She isn't dumb."

She looks at me, and I shake my head. "She's gonna be the death of me, Jakob! It's your turn to talk some sense into her."

I hold out my hand toward the hall. "I tried! She doesn't listen. She gets that from you."

"*Fix it!*" she screams, and then she comes undone. Elli must have said something, because Harper sneers, "I know I gotta let her fucking fly, Elli, but not with that shithead!"

I slowly back out of the room. If she'll yell at her best friend like that, she'll have no problem cussing at me. I'm an easy target, too. I made the kid with her. I shake my head as I start down the hall toward Allison's room. I should probably let the situation calm down, but I gotta head to the rink and I need her to hear what I have to say. I walk through the living room, and Journey hollers out, "May the force be with you."

I snort as I reach my daughter's room. I knock, and when she calls for me to come in, I take a deep breath. I'm terrified she is going to leave us. I push open the door to find her on her bed, looking down at a photo album. I close the door behind me, and she looks up at me with a tear-streaked face.

"I just want what y'all have. And if he leaves, I won't have that."

I scrunch up my face. "What?"

"You and Mom. I want that whirlwind romance that lasts lifetimes. And Taco, he's that for me."

"I don't understand," I say slowly before approaching the bed. It's then I see what she is looking at. The photo album of Harper and me when we first started dating.

She points to a photo. "We smile like this, and I swear he makes me laugh like this. It's all so picture-perfect."

I snort as I sit beside her. In the picture, I'm gazing at Harper like she's the queen of my world. She is, but man, I look like a doofus. "She ignored me for three days after that was taken."

She looks up at me, those eyes blazing into mine. "What?"

"Our romance wasn't picture-perfect, and we were older, Allison. That's what we're trying to tell you. Get your life together before you even try to find love, because it's rough."

"But...but y'all look so damn happy."

I nod. "In pictures, sure. But that doesn't show the times

she ghosted me, or the time we fought in the front yard, or how she would never commit to me. How I loved her more than she loved me for most of our relationship." I'm apparently rocking my child's world, but I feel I need to. "I'd have married her the moment I met her, but it took time for her to feel the same. Relationships are hard, love. So hard."

She seems put off by that. As if she doesn't believe me. I mean, based on these pictures, I wouldn't believe me either. "I thought you two fell in love right off the bat."

I snort. "No, I fell for her. But your mom...well, she was a free spirit, and man, if I didn't love that about her." I glance down at the book, taking one of the pictures of us out of it. "She tried to shake me so many times, and I wouldn't let her."

"See? So how can you want me to let go of Taco?"

Well, that backfired a bit. "Because while I wouldn't let her shake me, I also would never allow her to give up everything for me. I had her best interests in mind. Does Taco have yours?"

She looks down. I can see all over her face that he doesn't.

"Tell me."

I look over at her. "Tell you what?"

"Tell me the truth. Tell me what the pictures don't say."

I grin, my heart nearly exploding in my chest. I'm unsure if it's a good idea to tell my adult daughter our story, but my wife did tell me to fix it. I wrap my arm around her, kissing her temple before clearing the emotion from my voice.

"Well, one thing these photos don't show is the moment I fell in love with her."

"Or how he hit on me with the perfect confidence of a man who knew what he wanted."

I look up to see my wife in the doorway.

"He knew I was it. And all I was looking for was a good time."

"But I wanted more than just a good time."

Her eyes lock with mine, and it feels like it's more than twenty years earlier and I am falling all over again. "He wanted everything."

I nod, feeling Allison's gaze on us. "And I got it."

Harper's eyes darken, and my whole body explodes in flames. This woman. This life she gave me. Nothing could ever compare. "You gonna let me tell the story?"

She gives me a dry look, coming toward us and sitting beside Ally. "Have we ever done anything apart since then?"

Our gazes stay locked as I shake my head. "Never."

"Well, we won't start now."

My heart burns in my chest for this woman. "Are we censoring?"

Harper laughs, but Allison's face is full of horror. "Yes, please censor. I don't want to hear about y'all's sex."

Harper grins at me. "Fine. Plus, we know what happened."

Man, we sure do, and she will always be the best moments of my life.

NICE STICK

HARPER

T*wentysomething years ago…*

My best friend Elli Fisher would seriously lose her ass if it weren't attached.

She forgets everything and anything. She blames it on her thyroid, says it makes her forgetful, though I have a hard time thinking something the size of a butterfly can ruin so much. But I have seen it happen. I've watched my best friend gain so much weight so fast, and it wasn't like she was eating junk food. It all just happened, quickly, and because of it, I've watched her lose a man and her career over it. Elli being Elli, though, she fought back, lost the weight, and made a new career.

She's my idol.

We've been best friends since we were maybe five. We lived next door to each other, and then we shared an apartment in New York. I went to NYU for digital arts, and she was on Broadway. Man, those were the times. We partied, we laughed, and man, did we live. The men threw themselves at us, but Elli was committed to a fuckface named Justin, so I made sure to console all the men she rejected. I don't know what it is about a man, but hell if I don't love them. Relationships are for the birds, though. Elli is a good example of that, and I am A-okay without one. Love 'em and leave 'em is my motto.

As I haul ass through Luther Arena to meet up with Elli, I can't help but remember the times she would run across campus to bring me my camera or notebook. She is the ultimate best friend. We've been through so much together, good times and bad, and we'd die for each other. We always based our relationship off the one in *Sex and the City*. There are only two of us, but we might as well be four. I have enough personality for four women, and she has enough love. We're a pair, Elli and I. She's always dressed to the nines and looks perfect in her heels, while I'm lucky if I brush my hair. She budgets and likes control; I live on one hell of a prayer. She's insecure, and I'm so confident that it makes her confident. She's a romantic, and I just want to fuck.

But hell if I don't love her more than I do myself some days.

When I see her looking pristine as always, I grin as I wave the bulbs in the air. I cry out, "It's a madhouse out there!"

Elli is panicked. This is a huge thing for us. We're shooting the Nashville Assassins, our hockey team, and while yes, her uncle owns the team, this is the first time she's been asked to shoot for them. Believe me, we've applied like nine times, and I even asked Bryan Fisher over dinner once. He laughed at me. He doesn't take me seriously, though. I'll always be Elli's flighty, artsy-fartsy friend.

"I know. Come on! Let's go put in the bulbs."

I'm pretty sure she's five seconds away from curling up

and crying like a baby. She doesn't do well under pressure, and she loves the Nashville Assassins. The woman is probably the biggest fan I know. She has a room in her house dedicated to them. Her massive cow of a dog, yeah, he's named after the captain of the team. Which is good for me because I won trivia at the bar the other night because I knew his name. Sure as shit didn't know his first name, but I got the Adler part down and won fifty bucks for drinks. When I told Elli, she was disgusted that I didn't know Shea Adler's whole name and said she'd failed me. I now know his name is Shea Ryan Adler, he's twenty-nine, has a twin sister, is from Boston where he grew up with both parents, he's looking but hasn't found the one, and he's been the captain of the Nashville Assassins for three years. So, the next time there is Shea Adler trivia, I'm so winning.

Elli says something to some lady, but I'm off screwing in the bulbs. She's the talker of the pair. She oozes professionalism. I have purple hair, so, ya know, people don't take me seriously. I graduated at the top of my class with a major in graphic design and even have a minor in business studies. I think one of the rules is don't dye your hair crazy colors, but I tend to stay away from rules. I like being me, and I refuse to change that.

As I move to fix the lights and position them, I slip a little. The ice is a whole lotta slippery, but of course, it is ice. Duh. My heart is pounding, and I know it's because Elli is freaking out. She looks gorgeous with her auburn hair down in curls along her shoulders. She's wearing a cute little dress that hugs all her curves. After losing most of the weight she had gained, she was left with some killer curves. I don't have curves. Or breasts. But hey, I can suck a cock like no other.

I crouch down and open her bag to get out her camera. After attaching the right lens and making sure the flash is connected, I stand up to hand it to her. She takes it, but she doesn't smile or say thank you. I don't take offense. I'm just glad she's standing. "Go on over there and let me test-shoot, Harp."

I nod and quickly but carefully head to the spot we have marked for the players. Usually they do these in a black room, but I made the suggestion they should do it on the ice so it's more realistic. Bryan was appreciative of my artsy-fartsy self then. I pose with a stick, making sure not to smile since I don't think hockey players do. No teeth and all. I do it to make Elli laugh, but she's too nervous. I do get a small smile, though. When she looks down at the camera with a nod, I place the stick back and head toward her just as the guys start to come onto the ice.

Now, I am aware how gorgeous hockey players are. Elli has that room that shows off all of them, but there is a difference between seeing them on TV or in a picture and seeing them up close.

Big difference.

"Good golly, Miss Molly! Look at them. Good Lord. They are gorgeous," I whisper to her, and I can see she wants to die. If she weren't such a professional, I'm pretty sure she would have smacked me. Not that I would feel it, though. I'm too engrossed in each gorgeous man and his snazzy little jersey. The purple looks great on the guys, and the Assassin on the front with the Nashville skyline coming out of his shoulders is pretty badass. As I gaze at each of them, I realize I want to taste them all.

But then I notice a certain green-eyed devil checking me out.

Hell. Yes.

As each guy poses, I lean in as the amazing assistant I am. "For the love of God, El, that dude is hot."

She rolls her eyes. "Hush, Harp."

"No, really. Like, please, can I hit on one of them? Just one?" I don't know why I agreed not to hit on any of these fine men, but that was a really big mistake on my part. I want to be in an Assassins sandwich, covered and smushed by all of them.

"No."

She's so rude. "You're no fun."

She laughs it off, and that makes me happy. She's in her groove, unaffected by my crazy. When Green-Eyed Devil—also known as Number Two—comes off the bench with one hell of a smirk on his gorgeous face, I don't care what Elli wants me to do; I want him.

"Oh, to hell with what you say. Number Two is mine after this."

And there is no stopping me. Even with her pointed gaze, my eyes are locked with his. He's huge—I mean, like, smash a log with his bare hands huge, and I want to be that log. He's more than gorgeous; he's stunning. He has hard lines on his face, killer green eyes, and brown hair that is shaved up the sides and short on top. He looks like a Calvin Klein model, and I want to see him in nothing but those signature white undies.

"Hush, Harper!" Man, she full-named me. She usually calls me Harp. So rude.

Number Two should be looking at the camera, but those sexy eyes are on me. I run my tongue along my bottom lip, biting it gently as he takes in a sharp breath. In those green depths, I see nothing but the promise of a damn good time.

Yup, he's mine.

After his action shot of him shooting, looking like a biscuit I want to devour, he is supposed to head to the bench. But instead, he comes toward us. My body goes taut, my pussy tightens, and I swear, I can smell him from where I stand.

Then, he speaks.

"Nice hair, beautiful."

God, I'm coming home.

He may have knocked the air out of me, but I have my wits. I grin wildly at him, pushing back my shoulders so my tits look bigger than they are. "Nice stick," I say and then, very dramatically, run my eyes down his body and not to his stick but his *stick*. His eyes dance with excitement, and my body does the same. He skates off with a wink, and I am stoked. He is so becoming a notch on my bedpost.

Meanwhile, Elli is dying.

"You are impossible, Harper Allen."

And she wouldn't change a damn thing about me. She'd be so bored without me.

I actually feel the moment when Shea Adler hits the ice. It's crazy. I sense Elli go completely still. I can hear the air rush out of her, and when I glance at her, she looks as if she just saw Brad Pitt naked. I've never seen her stare at someone like that. Be so engrossed in them. I look over at where Shea Adler stands with his stick. He has the brightest blue eyes I have ever seen, and his almost-black hair only makes them bluer. He's one gorgeous man, but his nose is a little crooked. At least he has all his teeth, but…is he having a seizure?

"Why's he blinking so much?"

"Harp, shut up," she demands. But really, how is she supposed to take a picture?

He's trying to smile, maybe, or is he seizing up? "Is he hitting on you?"

"Oh my God!"

She is bright red, and I take great pride in that. She looks down, trying to gather herself, but once she sees all the pictures in her digital camera have his eyes shut, she realizes she'll have to tell him. She curses under her breath and then clears her throat. When I look back at the guy, he's rubbing his eyes.

"Mr. Adler," she says, all proper and cute. He tries to focus, but he's still blinking funny. "I'm sorry, but I need you to stop blinking. Your eyes are closed in every picture I have taken."

"I'm sorry," he says in one hell of a sexy Boston brogue,

and I think I hear Elli gasp. "I got new contacts, and they are bugging the hell out of me."

When someone hollers about getting him a new pair, Elli stands there completely stunned. It's actually funny to see. I almost expect her to drop to her knees to worship him. She has it bad for the guy, and to be honest, I think he thinks she's hot. "We can do the photos without them, right?" Before Elli can even utter a word, he's pulling his contacts out of his eyes. He throws them down on the ice, and when he looks up, it's easy to say he can't see. With a wide, devilish grin, he says, "I won't be able to see your beautiful face for a little bit, but I'll have a new pair soon. Then I can stare some more."

My best friend, God bless her, just stands there. Stunned in place. When she turns, her eyes are wide and her shoulders are taut. If we were at home, she'd be squealing like a sixteen-year-old, but Elli is too professional for that. Instead, she comes up beside me and gets to work. But I can feel the excitement pouring off her in waves, and I think something amazing is about to happen for her.

I hope so, at least. She needs it.

Elli is almost in a blur through the rest of the day. When it was time for the professional photos of the guys in suits, I took them. I flirted way more than I was supposed to with sexy Number Two, but Elli didn't say a word. Instead, all she did was mutter that Shea Adler called her beautiful. It's adorable and I want something to happen, but it's Elli. She doesn't go after guys. Hopefully Hottie McHottie will go after her.

It was a good day, and I'm proud of us. Elli is floating on cloud nine, and I feel damn good. This was successful; it can bring more business and, hopefully, some good sex. Shea for her, and Number Two for me.

We start to break down our equipment once we finish with the last guy. Elli is packing up the camera while I take the lights. I thought the room was empty except for her and me, but then I notice a huge body coming toward me. I slowly stand, a grin filling my face as his sexy ass approaches me. Like before, I can smell him, and desire swirls deep in my stomach. His green eyes are dangerous as they lock with mine.

"I couldn't leave without saying something to you," he says as he drops a huge bag at my feet. Is he being shy? How cute!

"Oh?" I ask, running my hands down my body and into my pockets. "What's that?"

He follows my hands with his eyes before meeting mine again. "That I need your number."

I scoff, playful and aloof. He was getting my number even if he didn't want it. "Is that right? You want my number?"

"I said need."

"Need, huh?"

"Yes," he says, and I can tell English is not his first language. Hell, it might not even be his second.

"I like your accent," I say, fluttering my lashes at him. "Where are you from?"

"Russia."

I wonder if we can play a dirty version of Russian roulette. Something where I don't know which hole he'll enter. That excites me. "It's sexy."

"You're sexy," he insists, and doesn't that make me hot everywhere. The way he says it, the way he is looking at me, like I'm the only person he sees, it actually takes my breath away. I look around the room and notice Elli isn't watching, nor is anyone else for that matter. When I glance back up at him, he's watching me. His eyes are so intent on mine, so dark. Wow. I swallow hard and wait for a sexy retort to come to me, but he's kinda knocked me on my ass here. "Well, I happen to think you'd be a real good time."

"Funny, I was thinking the exact same thing."

"So, I guess you do need my number."

"I do," he agrees, pulling out his phone, but his eyes still haven't left mine. "What is your name?"

Oh yeah, I forgot to ask that. I can't scream Number Two all night. Well, I could, but I'd rather know his name. "Harper."

"Harper," he says with a lot of sexy Russian flair. I mean, I like my name, but it's way hotter when he says it like that. "I'm Jakob. Jakob Titov."

I actually hear the K in his name. "Well, maybe I'll let you see my tits-ov."

His eyes dance with laughter before he chuckles. "That's funny."

"I'm a goofball."

He smiles… And wow, that's one gorgeous smile. He has all his teeth and they're straight; thank God for his dentist. "A sexy one."

"Well, yeah," I giggle, and he smiles.

"You'll call me?"

"I will."

"Today?"

"Maybe when I leave," I say, and I love that he wants me as much as I want him.

"I'd like that." He moves his eyes along my face, and I swear I can feel his gaze on my mouth. "You have very thick lips."

"Good for kissing and other things," I drawl, and his grin grows.

"I'd love to feel them."

"Oh yeah?"

"Yes."

Now, usually I'd go right for the mouth, but something has me going for his cheek. I lift up on my toes and give him a smacking kiss on his smooth skin. He groans loudly, backing away with his hand to his chest. He has this beautifully dazed look on his face, and I laugh. "Ah yes, very thick. I want more."

I can't stop laughing. "I'm not doing anything tonight."

"Yes, you are," he says simply, his eyes playful. "Me."

Well, smack my ass and call me Sally. He leaves me speechless as he gathers his bag and heads the other way. Oh, I am going to enjoy the shit out of him tonight. When Elli comes up beside me, I'm still watching him. "He'll call me when he gets to the car."

"How do you know? Did he say that?"

He didn't have to. He wants me. Bad. And he knows I want him. Why wait? "Nope, but he's needy."

I don't elaborate, and I don't have to. We both know I know my men. Jakob Titov puts on a real good show of only wanting one night, but I know his kind.

He'll want more. They always do.

But I'm not the one.

YOU CAME QUICK

JAKOB

I called Harper when I got to the car.

She didn't answer.

It was the first time a woman didn't answer my call. Usually when I ask for a number, they give it way too quickly and answer right away. Harper, though, nope. I called four more times and still no answer. I'm unsure what the hell happened between me getting the number and then walking away, but obviously, something did. I thought she was into me. I thought she wanted me like I wanted her. Maybe I got her number wrong? Damn it.

I stare at my phone as my best friend, Shea Adler, sits beside me. We're at his apartment, hanging out and drinking some beers. We had a long day, smiling for the cameras and discussing how awful that shit is. The only upside was seeing Harper's gorgeous face. Typically, I'm attracted to girls with huge breasts and long bleach blonde hair, the regular puck-bunny type. But today it was the girl with the bright purple hair in spikes. She intrigued me, and I really love her lips. I thought she liked all of me, too, so this is bullshit.

"Looking at the phone won't make it ring."

I don't even spare Shea a glance. "I don't understand. I thought she liked me."

"Maybe she was playing games. She looks the type, like a hard-core ballbuster," he says, bringing his beer to his lips. "I mean, I wouldn't be attracted to her."

I make a face. "No one asked you to be. Stay in your lane."

He grins. "Aw, you're already smitten."

I ignore him, staring at my phone. I would text her, but I suck at it, and that fucking autocorrect doesn't help at all. I'm not good with English words; I barely even speak them well. "You call her."

Shea pulls in his brows. "Who? The chick?"

"Yeah. Maybe she's ignoring me."

He looks at me, baffled. "So, why are we calling her?"

"She just needs to hear my voice, and I'll get her to talk to me."

"Yeah. No, stalker." When he laughs, I glare. He's supposed to be my best friend. "But can we discuss how fine that photographer was? Man, I was pissed when my contacts wouldn't stay in. She was something."

I shrug. When I was back home in Russia, she would be my type. A thicker woman who can make me some babies. Though, I can't help but remember the rich men being with model-thin women with big boobs. When I came to America, I felt that was how I would mark my success. Especially when I saw how wealthy American men were with their women. I'm actually surprised Shea likes the photographer. He is very much a blond, puck-bunny kind of guy. "She was very pretty."

"Yeah, and thick in all the right places." He grins like a kid with his hand in a cookie jar.

Wow, he does like her. "Totally different from who you've been with before."

I'm truly surprised he isn't settled down with a bunch of kids yet. He's a great uncle, and when we go to the Children's Hospital at Vanderbilt, it's as if all the kids are his. He's a leader, a good dude, and I'm lucky he's my best friend. He just doesn't do relationships. I can't fault him; most hockey players don't. We have grueling schedules, and we're gone a lot. It takes a special woman to deal with that. I really want Harper to be that special woman.

Shea shrugs, making a noncommittal face. "I think I'm done with that part of my life, those women. I want to settle down."

Now I'm the one making a face. Shea has never wanted to settle down. Like, ever. I've always wanted to settle down. Every woman I have dated has been because I'm looking for a wife, but it hasn't worked out for me. No one has wanted the same thing I do. But it was different with Harper. I felt that settling down feeling with Harper. I was aware I had only known her for maybe five minutes, but I felt it.

That spark.

But what surprises me is Shea feeling that feeling. Let's be honest... He likes women—a lot, actually—but I guess it has really slowed down the last couple years. Ever since he was selected captain. I think the pressure of setting an example is real for him, and then, his mom wants grandkids from him. She makes that known often. His last relationship didn't go really well, but it was all her fault. Shea is great. Good dude, loyal as hell. He just hasn't found the one. Maybe I didn't either. Shit.

"So, what has made you want to settle down?"

He takes a long pull of his beer and then smacks his lips. "I'm tired of it all. The sleeping around, the having to find a new chick when I want some. I don't just want to fuck—I want a companion. Someone I can share this life with."

I give him a pointed look. He basically said everything I have been saying. "When I said that, you laughed at me."

He grins, a wide, teasing one. "I was young and stupid then."

"It was a month ago."

Still grinning, he says, "I've grown so much."

"I think she would be perfect for you."

"Yeah?"

I clear my throat. "She looks like a good woman to make babies with."

Shea grins. "You always point out the baby-making women."

I smile. "It's all in the hips," I say with a wink. "Harper has nice hips."

He rolls his eyes as I lean back on the couch. "You just met her."

"And I felt something. Just like you did with photographer girl."

"True," he says slowly. "But I'm not waiting around for a call."

"Because you didn't give her your number or even get her name."

He pauses. "Touché."

I glance down at my phone to make sure it's working. It is, yet no call from Harper. "Should I call her again?"

"No!" he yells, and I realize I'm pouting. "Wait until the second half starts."

I look at the clock on the football game. Thankfully, I don't have long until I can call her. "So, are you going to go after the photographer?"

He nods. "Yeah, I called Grace to get me the info on her."

Ah, well, if he got his sister involved, then he's real serious. "Do you think she was interested?"

"Shit, I don't know. I sure hope so."

I nod. I want to think she was, but what do I know? I

thought Harper was interested, but instead, she's blowing me off. I had to talk myself down all day, reminding myself this isn't love at first sight. It can't be. But man, the rejection I feel right now... I'm thinking it might be. I've never had that happen, and for her to blow me off like this—shit, it hurts.

"Think Grace can find Harper?"

He laughs. "She'll call." I don't feel his confidence, but then my phone rings. When I see her name, I jump off the couch, fumbling with my phone to answer it. "Wow, dude. You're ridiculous."

I ignore him, taking a deep breath. "Hey, you."

She lets out a soft exhale. "Hey, I saw you called. A lot." She's teasing me, but I don't care.

"I did. I wanted to see you," I say, walking in a circle. Like, a literal circle. Just how a dog does it before he lies down to get comfortable. I want to get comfortable with Harper. And maybe a little uncomfortable. "I thought you wanted to see me, but you've been ignoring me."

She laughs breezily. "I was busy. I had to unload my stuff and then get back to my place."

"Oh, so you're home now?"

"I am."

"Did you want to go out?"

"I'd rather stay in."

My groin tightens at the promise in her voice. "I can bring food."

"I'd rather you just bring yourself."

She doesn't have to imply anything else; I am out Shea's door without even a goodbye.

And I'm not the least bit ashamed.

Harper had texted me her address, and when I pulled up to her little condo that looked more like a mini house than a condo, I couldn't get out of the car fast enough. I swear, the moment I heard her voice, I was ready to go. I feel as if I haven't gotten laid in years, when really, it's only been a few weeks. There is something about Harper, though, that has me feeling all dewy and new. When I reach her door, I tuck my phone into my pocket with my keys. I take a deep breath, and as soon as I knock on the door, she opens it.

And. She. Is. Butt. Ass. Naked.

Thank you, God. Thank you.

"Wow, you came fast."

My jaw actually drops. My heart jumps into my throat, my cock feels as if it's about to break off if I move, and all I can do is stare at the beauty in front of me. Her hair is wet, the purple from earlier gone. Her lashes are long as she looks up at me through them. Her body is trim, but those hips don't quit. Her lips are full, needing to be kissed, and I'm not one to hold back. I reach for her, wrapping my arm around her and yanking her into my chest. She comes hard into me as our lips meet in a heated and wanton embrace. If I thought her lips felt good on my cheek before, that is nothing to how they feel against mine now. Her body is hot underneath my fingers, and I can feel her heart beating in her chest as I drink from her succulent mouth.

Harper moves her fingers up my cheeks into my hair as she digs her nails into my scalp. I should take her inside, but I'm not finished kissing her. She runs her tongue along my lips, and when I open my mouth to hers, everything goes black. My heart nearly comes out of my chest, and I feel her on every nerve ending. She feels perfect against me, almost as if she were made to be pressed into me. I feel the warmth from the crux of her legs, and I want to bury my face in her.

I want to consume her.

When I pull away, it's not because I want to; it's because I can't breathe. Her blue eyes are blazing and astounding. Her lips are swollen from my kisses, and her body burns into mine. I am stunned by her. I cup her face, her jaw fitting real nice in my palm. I gaze into her eyes, wrapping my other arm tighter around her to hide her naked body. "Ah, *kiska*, you haven't seen anything yet."

She draws her brows together, and she seems a bit dazed. "Did you sneeze?"

"No. Come on, let me taste you."

I press my cock into her. It's throbbing, I want her so damn bad. She raises a brow and teases me more. "Are you going to disappoint me and come too quick?"

I shake my head, my gaze daring her to look away. "Oh no, *kiska*. You'll be the one coming too quick."

Harper's breath catches as her eyes search mine. "What are you waiting for?"

"The go-ahead."

Her eyes light up. "The go-ahead?"

"Yup."

She gives me a look, one I find I'm very fond of. It's somewhere between an "Are you kidding?" and "Please fuck me stupid." "I answered the door naked. That's your go-ahead."

I just grin. "Ah, *kiska*, so impatient."

Her eyes dance, and I can tell she wants to say something, but my mouth takes hers as we slowly back into her condo. When the door shuts behind us, I lift her up by her hips, her legs coming around my waist. I continue to kiss her as I scope out the room for a place to lay her down. The coffee table is a great spot, and when I set her down, her eyes travel along my body in the most satisfying way. I pull off my shirt as she sits up to undo my pants. Before they hit the ground, though, I grab my wallet, getting out my condom. I'm unsure who is removing my clothes faster, but soon, I am deep in her mouth. She brings me up on my toes, groaning loudly as she sucks me deep into that sweet mouth. Her thick lips cover me in all the right places. Soon, I see nothing but spots. I look down at her where she sits naked with my cock deep in her mouth.

She looks up at me through those lashes, and everything goes still.

This is the mother of my future children.

I cup her face as she moves up my cock, running my thumbs along her jaw as she continues to love my dick. I slide my hand down her body, caressing her breasts and then nipples, tweaking them and enjoying her sounds of pleasure. I trail my hand down to her sex, cupping it as I thrust into her mouth. She gags a bit but still sucks me hard. I dip a finger into her wet center and groan at the feeling. She's juicy as all fuck, and I want to suck her dry. Without much thought, I pull myself out of her mouth and drop to my knees before burying my face in her slick lips. She's bare, pink, and perfect in my eyes. She tastes like sweetness, and when she squeezes her thighs around my head, I breathe her in. A ragged noise leaves her lips as I suck her clit between my teeth. She arches up into my mouth, jerking against me as I continue to demolish her sweet pussy. I almost feel bad, but when she comes, hard and quick, gone is the guilt, replaced by pride.

"Fuck, you were right. I did come fast."

"And I'm not even done," I say against her perfect pussy. I kiss her once more before kissing up her pelvic bone and then her belly. I take her by the back of her knees and push them all the way up to her head. She's flexible, and man, if her pussy all wet and glistening up at me isn't a sight. She cries out as I press my body into hers, kissing her mouth. She deepens the kiss, her breathing so rough, and I love that I did that. That I am making her feel this. I thrust into her, and she engulfs my cock just the way I want. Everything goes white, and I can actually see the light vibrating.

I'm no saint, but this pussy right here, Harper's pussy, is the best fucking pussy I have ever been in. I brace myself against her legs, and I start thrusting into her. Hard. Our bodies slap together, her ass against my thighs, and I can't take my eyes off her. I pound into her and I hear something crack, but I'm too lost to care. Only a few more thrusts and I'm gone. I come so fucking hard my toes curl and my breathing stops. Everything around us goes still, and when I'm able to open my eyes, all I see is her. Her arms are above her head, her knees right there too. Her whole body is flushed, and her lips are parted in exhaustion. I lean into her, kissing her sweetly before slowly removing myself. I don't want to, but I'm pretty sure I broke her table. I reach for her, but she shakes her head.

"I can't move."

"Come on, *kiska*." I pull her up and notice we cracked the table. "Ah, I broke the table."

She looks over her shoulder and then back at me. "I think you broke me."

I grin, lifting her up into my arms. "Where is your bedroom?"

"That way, but I can go. You can leave."

I pull in my brows. "I'm not going anywhere."

"No?"

"No, I'm not done with you yet," I say, my eyes hooded and only for her. "I still need to fuck you from behind, I need you to sit on my face, I'd love to play with your ass, maybe get one hell of a blow job, and of course, eat you like a peach pie."

She actually looks stunned. "We're gonna get all that done in one night?"

I grin. "Sure."

Her eyes search mine. She's no longer broken or dazed. She's found her wits, and isn't that a shame. I liked her all wanton and lost for me. No worries, I'll get her there again. "You know this is a one-time thing."

I nod. "Sure, *kiska*."

She makes a face. "What is that? Kiska?"

"Means kitten," I say against her lips. "In Russian."

She seems a little breathless. "Well, that's hot."

"I'm pleased you like it."

She eyes me, and I can see the gears turning. She doesn't want to like me; she wants to use me. Too bad. "One night. That's it."

I just nod. "Sure."

She arches her brow. "I don't believe you."

I don't answer her. I take her mouth with mine and guide her back into her bedroom.

She has a good reason not to believe me, because I know this is not a one-time thing.

It's a forever and a day kind of thing.

OOPS, I DID HIM AGAIN...

HARPER

"I mean, jeez, El. Y'all need a room next time."

Elli stands against the wall, her hand to her chest and this euphoric look on her beautiful face. She looks adorable in a formfitting red dress that matches the bottom of her high-as-hell black pumps. When she called me to tell me Shea Adler had asked her out, I wasn't surprised. He had been giving her the eye. I think I'm more excited than she is. I want this for her. A great new relationship that can show her her worth. I believe Shea can do that; I am usually good with reading guys. I stay away from guys like Shea, but then I fucked up and let Jakob into my bed...

Sigh.

Shea had shown up at the studio in the middle of the day and convinced Elli to go to lunch with him. She didn't need much convincing, though. I know for a fact that she is completely infatuated with him. Which is very much the opposite of me. I am in no way thinking of Jakob. I sure as hell don't care what he is doing. Or even want to see him.

He was a one-time thing.

A one-time thing that I realized may have somehow happened a second time—and I am still very confused how I let that happen—but still a one-time thing. I shouldn't have opened the door the second time, but no guy had ever just shown up. Jakob didn't care that I had been ignoring him for three days. He didn't have any cares at all that I didn't want to see him. All he said was, "I want to see you, *kiska*."

It's that damn *kiska*. It gets me every time he says it. I love it. No one has ever given me a sexy nickname, and I was blinded by it. I yearn for it, but it doesn't matter. He can't happen. We won't happen again. Nope. I am single and ready to mingle with anyone but Jakob Titov.

Elli looks over at me, shaking her head. This dreamy, beautiful look is on her flushed face. "He's fantastic."

I grin, nodding. "I'm aware."

I hear a bit of resentment in my voice that shakes me to my core. I don't understand it. Elli must have not heard it, because she comes toward me, falling very dramatically into the chair in front of my desk. "He makes me feel so many things. Deep inside. He makes me laugh. He gives me butterflies. Harper, the way he kisses… I mean, he is just perfect," she coos, and I ignore the thought that Jakob might be perfect, too. I mean, he fucks like an absolute dream. He kisses like I am the only thing he wants to taste. When he smiles at me, something in my stomach flip-flops and does a damn twirl. We didn't speak much; we were too busy tasting every single inch of each other, but I wouldn't mind getting to know—

What in the world? I don't get it. I don't get crushes on guys. I don't care enough to, which is why I have to stay away from him. I might start to care.

That cannot happen.

"How's Jakob?" she asks with a dreamy smile. She looks like she should have little hearts and rainbows flying around her.

"I don't know," I say a bit harsher than I intended to. I swallow hard, trying to gather myself. "I haven't talked to him."

I feel her staring a hole in the side of my face. "Why? I thought y'all slept together again. He was all about it."

"He is. I'm not."

"What? Why?"

"Because I don't want to be."

"Why?"

"Are you a parrot? Leave it be. Nothing is going to happen. One and done."

"You did him twice. A lot. Like, all night."

I flash her a dark look. "I know, and I don't need that reminder. I just need to forget him."

"Wh— I mean, ugh… I don't understand."

I exhale very loudly. "I'm not a one-man woman. Too many dicks, too little time."

"Oh, Harper. Come on. It's me."

I still won't look at her. I am editing a first birthday shoot I did last week. The photos are adorable and way more interesting than this conversation. "Well, since it's you, you know I don't want to get involved with someone just for them to hurt me."

She lets out a soft noise. Sounds very sympathetic to me, which kind of pisses me off. "I know you didn't have the greatest luck in high school—"

Greatest luck? Is she delusional? "You mean every guy I dated cheated on me? Thanks for the reminder, El."

I look over at her just as she snaps her lips together. "To be honest, you didn't really pick good guys."

I shrug. "So? I thought I was enough."

"You can't be enough for someone who won't value your worth." Elli says the words so confidently. Something I haven't heard from her in a very long time. I almost scream out in joy, but then I remember what we're talking about.

I bring in my brows. "Those are some pretty big claims for someone who says Shea Adler couldn't be into her."

A small smile pulls at her lips. "Maybe I'm opening my eyes, and maybe you should too. I hear Jakob is amazing."

He is. I mean, the sexual and cuddling side of him is. I don't know any other side. "I don't even know him."

"You could try."

I shake my head. "Like I said, he's needy. One of those guys who wants to get married and make babies. I am not that woman."

"You could be."

I glance back at her. "Please. No one has ever looked at me and thought that."

Her eyes are kind. "I do. I always have. Especially when you're with my nieces and nephews. You're the life of the party. Always."

I look away, shrugging. I've never seen that in my future. Hell, let me be honest and say I never thought a man would want me for more than a night.

Then entered Jakob Titov.

"I don't know."

"I've never in my life seen you scared of something."

I scrunch up my face. "Ugh, I made you kill that spider the other day."

She laughs. "You know what I mean."

I lick my lips since they're becoming irritably dry. "I don't know. He makes me nervous."

"Scared, you mean."

I shake my head. "I'm not scared of some dude. I won't give anyone the power to hurt me, which is why I'm staying away."

"But you want to."

"Want to what?"

"Give him that power."

I mean, it wouldn't be horrible, but I'm not admitting that. "No way."

"I know you, Harper Allen, and I think he likes you a lot. I also don't think he is going anywhere."

I side-eye her. "I kicked him out of the apartment and slammed the door in his face."

"But he's called."

"So?"

"And you've ignored him?"

"Yeah."

"I don't think he cares about that."

"Why would you say that?"

She nods toward the front door. "He just got out of the car with a really big bouquet of flowers."

I whip my head to the front, and sure as shit, he's standing in the parking lot. He has a huge bouquet of roses in his hand wrapped in brown paper with a white bow. He has on some really nice-fitting pants and a pressed button-down shirt. His dark hair is brushed to the side, and he's clean-shaven, unlike the other night. He pushes his sunglasses up into his hair and looks toward the shop. He can't see us—the windows are tinted—but I can see him.

And. Wow.

"You gonna run? He's coming in."

I stand up, fixing the front of my shirt so my breasts look good. I pull up my jeans and jerk my thumb to her office. "Vamoose, you."

She laughs as she gets up, heading back to her office just as the door opens and Jakob enters. "Hey, Jakob," she calls over her shoulder. "Good luck."

I'm gonna kill her. I look back at him, and he's only looking at me. His green eyes burn my skin as he takes me in. He clears his throat. "I've been calling you."

I press my lips together, tucking my fingers into my back

pockets. "Yeah, I've been ignoring you. I told you this couldn't happen."

He nods slowly as he closes the distance between us. "I don't take 'no' very well."

I love his voice. Breathlessly, I gaze up into his gorgeous eyes. "I am discovering that."

"I got these for you," he says, handing me the over-the-top bouquet. It looked smaller when he was outside. Now that it's in my hands, I'm sure there are at least five dozen roses. "I've thought of you this many times since I bought them, and I don't care if that's corny. Shea said I was corny."

I grin, puckering my lips as I run my finger along the bow. "Just a bit. But it's also incredibly sweet of you." I look up, and he's dropping his lips to mine. I should push him away, I should dodge his kiss, but I fall into it. He brings his hand up, holding my jaw as our lips move together.

When he pulls back, he's only a breath away before he says, "Don't pucker those lips unless you want to be kissed, *kiska*."

Fucking hell.

I'm lost in his eyes as I gaze up at him. "Take me to dinner."

"Okay."

"And this is it. I'm going to see if I like you, and if I don't, you'll have to let me go."

"Okay."

I glare. "You're not going to let me go."

He slowly shakes his head. "Nope, because you're going to love me."

And for the first time, I realize I am actually scared.

I'm petrified he is right.

With how hot he looks, I expected him to take me to some

fancy restaurant, but instead, we go to a hole-in-the-wall taco place. Don't get me wrong—it's the best tacos in Nashville, but I thought only I knew about this place. Even Elli doesn't like it. She says she feels like they get the tacos off the floor. I don't care where they get them; they taste like heaven, which is why I ordered ten of them. Plus, they're small. Like, two make one, so in all reality, I got five. Still a normal and decent amount.

But I still say, "Don't judge me. I'm hungry."

He grins as he gestures toward me. "I'll take ten of the same."

The waitress nods and walks off. I cross my legs and then uncross them before recrossing them again. I'm flustered, but Jakob sits across from me, cool as a cucumber with a sneaky little look on his face. "What?"

"You look beautiful. I love your hair like that."

I reach up, touching my hair. I have it gelled down in the front and wild in the back. It's my "I was too lazy to do anything with it" style. "Well, thanks. I basically rolled out of bed this morning. I was up late—" I stop quickly, looking down at the table. I was up late because I kept tossing and turning, thinking of his fine ass.

"What were you doing, other than ignoring my calls?"

I look up, a grin pulling at my lips. "Just watching TV."

"Should have called me, I would have come over and watched with you."

I taunt, "Please, you'd want more."

"Really, no. I just want to be near you." His accented English sends my heart into a frenzy. "I feel you like to be near me too."

I shrug. "I mean, it's not horrible."

He chuckles softly. "So, do you have family?"

He's completely unfazed by my resistance. I don't know if it's confidence or if he doesn't understand I don't want this.

I don't.

I really don't.

Right?

"I do," I find myself saying. "My mom and dad, and I have a set of twin sisters. They're younger."

He nods. "Nice. I have a brother, but our parents are our adoptive parents. We were adopted when I was a bit older, but my brother Erik is younger."

"Does your brother play hockey?"

He smiles up at me. "Yes, he is very good. Some would say better than me. Not my mom, though. She says we are both the best."

"Sounds like something my mom would say. She gushes over all of us, when we all know I'm her favorite."

He laughs, and I can't help but grin. "Ah yes, my mom does the same. My real parents, not so much. My mom ran off without us, and my dad was very… Uh, what is the word? Mean? No, something worse—"

"Abusive?"

He nods, pointing to me as our tacos are set down in front of us. "Yes, abusive. He hurt us terribly, but we are okay now." He digs into his tacos like he didn't just tell me something very personal. I don't think I would ever tell someone something like that unless I truly knew them. He just met me.

He knows my vagina better than he knows me.

"I'm so sorry."

He waves me off. "In the past. I have a good future ahead of me."

Wow. His resilience is really sexy. "Is that right?"

"Yup. You're in it," he says around a mouthful of his food. "Remember, you're gonna love me after tonight."

I laugh, though I can't ignore the clench in my stomach. "Cocky much?"

"Always," he says with a wink. "You always want to be a photographer?"

I bite into my taco and nod. "I did. I went to NYU for it."

"What is NYU?" he asks slowly.

"Oh, you didn't grow up here?"

He laughs. "Doesn't my accent give me away? I grew up in Russia."

I feel dumb. "Yeah, duh. I don't know, I thought maybe you came here when you were adopted."

"I did, but I was already fourteen, and my parents know Russian, so we hardly spoke English. But yeah, I know it all now. I forget sometimes, but the written word gets me."

"Can you not read in English?"

"Not much. I try, though," he says with a wry smile. "It's hard, but I learn."

"I don't doubt it," I say, and then I smile. "I could help."

Why. In. The. Hell. Did. I. Say. That?

I quickly add, "You know, if we make it out of this, both of us wanting to."

He gives me a dry look. "You don't believe this, huh?"

"Believe what?"

"This feeling. I feel it. You do, but you're ignoring it."

"I am not. I mean, I don't feel anything. You're a fantastic lay and I have fun, but I don't date."

"You don't date? Why?"

"Guys are assholes."

He nods. He's already eaten four tacos. "Some are, but I'm good."

I can't help but grin at him. "Man, now I think you're full of yourself."

"I am," he says with no apology. "I spent many years thinking I was not good enough. I don't do that anymore. I gotta live each day fully, because they can be taken away, like this," he says, snapping his fingers. "I have a good life. I want to make it better. Do you feel like that?"

"Huh?" I ask, confused. "Feel what?"

"That you want a better life. You have a good life, yeah?"

I shrug. "It's okay."

I mean, I live a good life. I work my ass off to make the studio successful, I sleep with whomever I want, I see my family when I want, and I do what I want. It isn't bad. Do I want more? Sure. But I don't really know what that means. I don't like being lonely; I find myself at Elli's house or even my parents' more than I care to admit. I don't do things alone; I always go with Elli, but now that she is with Shea, she's busy with him. Maybe I need a dog? No, way too needy. A cat. Cats aren't needy.

But from the way Jakob is looking at me over the tacos he's devouring, I suspect he thinks he belongs in the void I didn't know I had.

"Then you want better," he says simply, eating like this is a normal, day-to-day conversation. Lord, he's flipping intriguing. "Don't you?"

I look at my taco, tearing off a piece before popping it into my mouth. "Yeah, sure."

"I thought so. Do you like movies?"

I eye him. "Yeah, why?"

"We should go to one. Thursday. I have a game tomorrow."

"Oh. Um—"

"I'll pick you up at six," he says, watching me. "And you can tell me about this NYU."

I look away shyly. "It's a college."

He nods. "That's a big school?"

Why am I turned on by the fact that he doesn't know that? "Yeah, I graduated from there."

"Ah, okay. Wow, that's awesome. You're very smart, then?"

I grin. "I'm all right."

"I bet you are very smart. I will need to take you up on helping me learn." He winks, and my heart skips a beat. I want to help him and also slam my face into the table. I'm unsure which will lead to more pain. "So, we go?"

Should we go? I'm sure Elli will be with Shea, and then I'll be at home with my computer. We have no events this week, not until Saturday and Sunday, and everything is during the day. I mean, there is really no reason not to go. I like him well enough. He's damn cute, and I like having sex with him. Something that could really make my week.

"Only if you take me home."

His eyes stare into my soul. "I was going to."

"I mean tonight."

He nods, so fucking confident and gorgeous. I can see his chest puffing up, the passion in his eyes. Hot damn if he doesn't turn me on. "I was going to."

Breathlessly, I bite my lip. "Then, yes."

"And I'll stay."

"Stay?"

"Yes. I have a bag in the car."

I wait for the freak-out to come. The flight sense. But it doesn't appear. Instead, I can only feel sheer desire. "Who said anything about needing a bag?"

He grins. "My breath is awful in the morning."

I can't help but grin back at him. "Is it?"

"You'll see," he says, polishing off the rest of his taco. "Now, eat up so I can eat you up."

Oh man, I need to keep my wits about me with Jakob Titov before he knocks me clean on my ass.

Something no man has ever done.

IT'S BEEN A WEEK

JAKOB

"**D**ude, you're always talking to her. She's going to think you're desperate."

My way of thinking is this—I tease him so he realizes his feelings. I love Shea, but he's a bit dense. He's used to being all about himself. I want him to see that now, he's all about a woman.

"No, she won't. I just like talking to her," he says defensively as he dries his balls. "So, shut up."

I grin. Exactly what I wanted him to say. I want him to get defensive. I want him to fight for what he wants. When you're the captain of a National Hockey League team, women tend to throw themselves at you. Shea has a plethora of women doing that. "You've seen her every day since Sunday. You are smothering her!"

His eyes narrow to slits. "I am not! And this coming from the guy who's basically stalking what's her name."

Now, I'm glaring. I talk about Harper enough for him to know her name. Plus, he's dating her best friend. Elli loves

Harper; I'm sure she talks about her too. "Harper, but I love her. It's different."

His jaw drops, and I know I've surprised him. But really, the only thing I'm surprised by about my comment is that he didn't realize it. I mean, I've only talked about Harper all day and all night. On the ice, off, all the time. The girl is it for me. She makes me absolutely senseless, and I love how proud she is. I love how she doesn't give a fuck what anyone thinks. She just does Harper, and that turns me on. I want a girl who loves herself and knows her worth. I really appreciate the fact that she is making me work for her. I don't want it to be handed to me. Yeah, she gave me her body, but I'm working for her heart. I'll get it. I'm wearing her down, and it really excites me. I want her to know what I know and fall completely and utterly in love with me.

Shea, though, he doesn't seem to be processing what I've just said. "Oh my God. Really, dude? It's been a week!"

I smile proudly, confidently. "I know the one when I see her."

He seems very confused by me as he stands, wrapping a towel around his waist. "You know what? Before you try to give me advice on how to date girls, get your love life squared away."

As he walks away, I say, "I got my life squared away. I'm in love with an NYU graduate who is beautiful and smart, and I'm not the least bit embarrassed to say so."

Shea looks over his shoulder at me. "You're insane. That girl doesn't even have you on her radar."

I'm offended. "The fuck she doesn't. I'm all over that."

Shea rolls his eyes, shaking his head as he leaves to go to wherever he is going. I'm unsure of his destination, but I'm dressed and ready to go. I say bye to some of the guys. I look forward to seeing them tomorrow. We play tomorrow, and I'm hoping I can convince Harper to come. I want her to see my second love. To know what makes me tick. I'd love for her to meet my parents, but I'm just lucky she didn't kick me out of her bed the last couple mornings. To my surprise, I haven't left her condo much. Only for the rink and when we go places together. It's been really nice. Normal for me. The normalcy I crave. After such an awful childhood, I want love and a life that is worth living. I didn't get my parents until later than I needed. I wish I'd had that example my whole life, the way they love each other. But thankfully, I didn't need long to catch on.

Harper and I can be what my parents are. I just need her to get on board.

When I push open the side door that leads to the players' parking lot, I feel a slow grin cover my lips when I see Harper leaning against my car. She's wearing a tight gray sweater dress and heeled black boots. She hasn't put the purple color back in her hair since we've been talking, and I don't think I miss it. I love her hair, dark and styled to perfection. When she smiles, though, everything else fades away.

Every single word I said from before about Harper rings true. I love her.

I love her so damn much.

I don't say anything as I close the distance between us. When I circle my arms around her waist, she comes up against my chest, wrapping her arms tightly around my neck. "Hey, you," she says against my lips just as I drop them to hers. I kiss her, feeling every single emotion well up inside of me. I don't know what she is doing here, and to be honest, I don't care one bit. I'm just glad she's here. She pulls back first, grinning as she runs her thumbs along my cheeks. "Well, hot damn, I'll wait for you more often if that's the way I'm greeted."

Ah, I love her country accent. Elli's is way more out there, but Harper's hits me in the feels. I squeeze my arms around her, kissing her top lip. "I want it to be every day."

She giggles against my lips, leaning into me. "Stop. You're making me blush."

"Good," I say, kissing her cheeks that have filled with color. "Tell me you've come by to go to dinner with my parents?"

She laughs against my nose. "No way. Came to make you take me to lunch, and you said you'd replace my coffee table. It broke the rest of the way today."

I grin before reaching out to my Jeep to open the back. She tears her gaze from mine to look inside and find the exact coffee table we broke the first night we were together. She looks up at me with a dreamy expression. "Or we can get takeout and go back to my place to put this together."

"And maybe break it again?"

Her eyes darken and sparkle with desire. "Maybe."

"I love that word."

"Yeah?" I nod, and she bats her lashes at me. "Maybe I'll do that thing you like."

My groin tightens, and I am well aware what she is speaking of, but I need more. "Like come to my game tomorrow?"

I'd say she is surprised by my question, but she recovers well. "Your game?"

"Yeah, tomorrow at seven. I can get you tickets—"

She moves her fingers through her hair. "Elli has tickets. She's been begging me to go to a game."

I lean into her, pressing my nose against the side of hers. "Can I beg you?"

She looks at me through her lashes. "Maybe."

Ah, that word. From those lips. "I want you there. I want you to see how passionate I am about my work. When you showed me your photos, I was amazed by your talent. Let me amaze you."

She takes a deep breath. "You already do." Oh, the grin on my face is unstoppable, and she smiles shyly as she slides her fingertip along my jaw. "Which is why you've woken up beside me with that awful breath."

I laugh. "And I appreciate you for dealing with my breath. But let me show you what else I can do."

Her eyes meet mine, and she nods slowly. "It doesn't mean anything if I go. Like I keep saying, we aren't together."

I roll my eyes. Yes, she has said this a time or two, and no, I don't believe her at all. "What did I tell you about that? I don't want to hear your lies."

"I'm not lying. We're not together. We're just dating."

"So, does dating mean we spend every night together for a week?"

She looks away. "Sure does."

"And it means that I hold you for hours on end while we watch all those weird, scary shows you like?"

She won't look at me. "*Supernatural* is not scary."

"It is too, which is why I hold you."

She shrugs. "Fine, yes."

"And tell me... Dating means we stay up all night talking and learning more about each other, naked, in bed."

She finally meets my gaze, that determined look on her face that drives me wild. "Those are all details that don't need to be mentioned. Especially the naked one."

I grin with a wink. "But the naked part is my favorite."

"See, which is why we're dating, maybe even fucking."

I shake my head. I hate that more than the "we're just dating" bullshit. "No, we left all that behind when I learned the names of your family, your friends, and how many men you slept with before me. We—me and you—are doing something here, Harper. Admit it."

"No way," she says, very resistant. "Never."

"You're going to admit it," I promise her, and she presses her lips together. "And you're coming to my game to cheer me on because you want to watch me win."

"Or I'm coming to the game because I want to hang with

my friend." I give her a dry look, and she sends me one right back. "Don't rush me, Jakey."

I laugh from the gut, despite her annoyed look. "But you've given me a nickname and we're only dating?"

She glares as her face warms with color. It's so beautiful, the color, but on her, it's breathtaking. "Hush."

"Never. I will get you to admit this is more than just dating."

She rolls her eyes. "I won't."

"You will, and when you do, it's gonna blow us both away."

She narrows her eyes. "This will probably end before that could ever happen."

I laugh. "This is never going to end." She rolls her eyes, and I look at her seriously. "Why would you say that?"

"Because things don't last."

"This will."

"How do you know?" she asks mutinously.

"Because I feel it, just as you do. But you choose to ignore it."

She sets me with a pointed look. "I don't feel anything."

"You can say that all you want, but I feel it in your kiss," I say, moving my thumb along her lip. "In the way you look at me. The way you hold me. And most definitely the way you smile."

Her eyes soften, and her lips quirk at the side. "People don't stay with me."

"Do you give them a chance?"

She stares at me, her eyes burning into mine. "I don't have to."

"Well, give me the chance, Harper, because I'll prove you wrong. Over and over again," I promise, taking her mouth with mine. I know she probably has a lot to say to that, but thankfully, she falls into the kiss.

Just like how I want her to fall in love with me.

Just like how she *will* fall.

I know it.

When I come onto the ice, the first thing I see is Harper.

She's wearing a purple jersey, and I'm pretty sure I see a number two on each of her cheeks, but I won't get my hopes up. She has her hair spiked tonight with the purple throughout it. She's wearing bright purple eye stuff and even lipstick. Her style excites me. Like her best friend, who is wearing every piece of Shea Adler merchandise there is, respectively, Harper looks as if she is a fan, but I know that's not the case. Or at least, that's what I've been told. This is the first game she's ever been to. And I don't care what she says; she's here for me. I didn't know where Elli's seats were, but to any hockey fan, they're badass. Right beside the penalty box and immediately across the ice from where we come out.

As I put a puck to my blade, I watch as Shea skates right for where Elli and Harper are sitting. Even though no one can tell, I watch as he talks through the glass to Elli, who looks more like a teenager than a grown woman. She is excited and basically bouncing while looking at Shea. She is all about him, and Shea is eating it up. Harper sits beside Elli with this look of disgust on her face, and it annoys me. I want her to be excited like that for me, but her words from earlier taunt me. She hasn't even looked at me. Fine, two can play at that game.

I move the puck back and forth as I skate with my team. I love warming up; it gets the blood going, and I usually know how I am going to feel throughout the game from the twenty-minute warm-up. I love seeing the fans, especially the kids. I never got to go to games when I was a kid. My birth father was too busy beating the shit out of my brother and me, and my birth mom was off doing something other than raising us. Or protecting us. When my parents came to save us, I stayed scared for about three years, and then finally, I started to come into my own. Sometimes, I feel it was easier for me to let go because it wasn't as bad for me as it was for Erik. Our birth dad really hated Erik, and I think it was because he looked so much like our birth mother. I favored our birth father. But seeing the kids here only fuels me to have my own and love them how I wish Erik and I had been loved before our parents came for us.

I move around the goal, and I stand there grabbing pucks and throwing them up and over the glass. Kids squeal, parents smile in gratitude, and it makes me feel a certain way. Out of the corner of my eye, though, I notice Harper is watching me. Her brow is furrowed and she looks pissed, but I don't pay her any mind. While we had a great afternoon and even a great night when I went back to her place after my dinner with my parents, her claim of our not being together is still annoying me. I know the truth, but it bugs the shit out of me that she is holding so tightly to her insistence on not giving us the label we deserve. I get that we don't need a label and I'd probably be better off by not putting one on us, but I already told my parents she's the one.

And I won't be wrong.

I know I'm not.

When Shea hollers out, "Break!" I haul ass to the blue line as we start our drills. We do them every warm-up, and they bring us together. We rush the net and then go to the blue line. We do these many times before our goalie takes his position and we start shooting on him. Word is this is his last year, but I'll believe it when I see it. Liyamia has been here longer than Shea and me combined. Who could possibly replace him?

As I watch my teammates, I move my feet quickly, taking in deep breaths. My parents are up in the stands along with Erik, who flew in to watch. He's still playing for the Philadelphia Flyers' farm team, but he's gonna make it soon enough. I feel it. He's a badass player. As I look up toward the box my parents should be in, I can't see them, but I know they're there. They don't miss warm-ups. When it's my turn to shoot, I crash the net and I take a good shot, going five-hole before skating off to the right where Harper and Elli are sitting. I look up to find Harper watching me.

I can't help it. I smile before jutting my chin toward her. She stands up, a grin on her face before she turns for me, showing me the Number Two jersey she wears. She then points to the side of her face where my number is painted on her cheek, and everything inside of me goes hot. I send her a wink, my heart in my throat, and she blows me a kiss. I purse my lips to her, wishing mine were against hers. I know it's not professional, but I sure as fuck don't care. As she lowers back into her seat, admiration all over her gorgeous face along with a lot of excitement, I can't help but laugh at her words.

Her claims.

I don't get why she is so resistant to me. So, she's been hurt. Yeah, it sucks. But I'm not them. I'm me. And I am everything she needs and wants. I know it's only been two weeks since I met her, but I swear I knew the moment I saw her. A confident, loud, wild woman with a smile that knocks me on my ass? Yes, that's who I want. Who I need. Who I see as the mother of my children. I've seen how she speaks of Elli's nieces and nephews, how much she loves her own sisters, and I want that kind of love for myself. For our children. After seeing my number on her, that smile as she danced just for me, I know for a solid fact that Harper is who I see my life with. And she's gonna see it too. I will get that woman to fall for me because that's what she deserves. A life with a good man who will erase what those other fuckers did to her.

Who will love her for her loud, stubborn, gorgeous self.

I'm that man.

HARPER

I am doing something I swore I would never do.
I am missing a man.
Desperately.

Figures the first guy I allow myself to miss really fucks with me. I find myself wandering into Elli's office. She was on the phone before, but now she's doing whatever on the computer. She doesn't even seem to care Shea is gone. Really confusing to me since they spend every waking moment together. I worry she's going to ruin this because of her insecurities. But really, am I one to talk? I won't even admit to what I'm feeling for Jakob. What we are. I know it's gonna really piss him off one of these times, and I may lose him.

I fall face first into Elli's couch, groaning.

The thought of losing him hurts my chest.

"What the hell is wrong with you?"

I roll over onto my back, inhaling deeply. "I miss sex!" I mean, I can't come out and tell her the truth. She'll make assumptions, and I can't have that. Love is a weakness...and that way of thinking makes no damn sense since I want her to fall in love and be happy. Why don't I want that for myself? I deserve that. I'm a good person. So, what makes us different?

"What do you mean? You can have sex with anyone," she says offhandedly, like it's nothing. *Go out and fuck someone else, Harper. It isn't like Jakob is important to you.*

I sit up quickly, and I notice she leans back in her chair and it rolls back. "If you laugh, tell anyone, or even smile, I'll throw something at you!"

She looks at me wryly but says, "Okay."

I swallow hard past the lump in my throat. This is my best friend, and maybe if I show some emotion, she'll realize her feelings, and boom, she'll get what she always wanted. A good man who loves all of her, even the parts she doesn't. "I miss sex with Jakob. I miss…him."

I can see it all over her face. She wants to cry out in celebration, cuddle me to her bosom, and tell me how happy she is. Instead, she covers her mouth and mutters, "Oh."

I throw up my arms, feeling disgusted with myself as I drop my head back. "I've never in my life had this problem, but that damn Russian brought his big ole penis into bed with me, and now no other man even measures up. I miss my Jakey!"

Out of nowhere, tears roll down my face. I look over at Elli for help, but I think she's as stunned by my tears as I am. "I don't know what my problem is. I never get like this with guys. I just miss him, you know? Don't you miss Shea?" I find myself asking, needing some kind of explanation for my emotional outburst.

Maybe I'm about to start my period?

"Oh yeah," she agrees, her eyes kind. "But I'm in a relationship with him."

This bitch. I'm supposed to be helping her admit her feelings, not being forced to admit my own!

"Well, yeah. But I mean, I don't know… I just miss Jakob."

When her lips curve, I glare. I know what I sound like, and I refuse to be pitied! "You're smiling!"

She isn't listening to me, though. An email has come in, and then she's watching some music video. So I head out of the room, wiping my face. I don't understand what I'm feeling. It's all a rush. All so confusing. As I head to my desk, I hear the song restart, and I assume it's from Shea. Who else would send her a song about needing just a kiss from her? Shea is all about Elli, and it's adorable. So why do I fight how much Jakob is about me? I'm going to push him away and I really don't want to do that, but I also don't want anyone to know I don't want that.

Yes, I am aware I'm a basket case.

When I fall into my desk chair, I find myself reaching for my phone. I dial his number, and when his low, thick Russian accent fills the line, I find myself sighing.

"Hey, *kiska*."

Kiska.

I swoon. Like, literally swoon. I'm two seconds from clutching my heart like he did the first time we met. "Hey, what are you doing?"

"Lying in bed, playing on my computer. Shea and Elli are flirting and being disgusting, so I'm ignoring him."

I grin. "Was that him who sent the video?"

"Oh yeah. I think the song is stupid. I want more than just a kiss."

"Oh, really? A kiss isn't enough?"

His voice is deep and sexy. "No, I want all of you."

I take in a sharp breath. "Oh."

"Yeah. If you were the kind of woman who would be receptive to music, I would spend hours finding the right song."

Fuck, he leaves me breathless. "Maybe I am."

"Yeah?"

"No," I say quickly, and then I smack myself in the fore-head. "I mean, yeah. No. Hell, I don't know."

He pauses, and I can hear him move in the bed. "What's wrong, *kiska*?"

I cover my face with my hand, exhaling on a rush. "I don't know, Jakob. I miss you."

I can actually hear the smile in his voice. "I miss you, my love."

His love. Ugh. "I don't want to hurt you. I don't want this to end. I feel like I'm pushing you away with my own fucked-up way of thinking, and I don't know how to fix that. But I've been hurt left and right, and that's why I keep men at arm's length. But apparently, you don't care about that and keep coming for me, and I don't want to fuck this up. I don't want to hurt you or lose you." I take in a deep breath. "I really don't understand it either, 'cause my parents are happy and my sisters are in healthy relation-ships. And then there's me, being all weird about being in a relationship. I think I want to be in one, but I don't. I don't know."

He doesn't say a word. He lets me word-vomit, and soon, I am gasping for breath as I hold the phone to my ear. "Jakob?"

"Don't speak, my love. I don't want to hear this stuff, because nothing that is easy is worth it. I want this to be hard for you, because when you give in, you'll truly give in to me." He leaves me shaking with fear. But a good fear. Not the scary kind. Jakob's voice is so welcoming, so confident as he says, "If you're gonna take the chance, if you're gonna hurt anyone, do it to me. And when we fall, blame it all on me, because that's what I want. I want you to fall head over heels in love with me and ruin all men because of how much you love me. I want you, only you, Harper."

I press my lips together as I close my eyes. "Okay."

"Okay," he says, and I swear his face is bright with happiness. I don't have to see it to know it's true. "Can I take you away when I get back?"

"Away?"

"Yes, I want to go away, just us. No distractions."

I lick my lips. There is no answer other than "Yes."

When Jakob said he wanted to take me away, I really didn't think he was serious about the no-distractions part. He was. We're in the middle of nowhere, and I'm pretty sure the only signs of life here are bears. I've never been to Gatlinburg before, but it's beautiful. Stunning, really, but I wish there were a Target around. The closest thing is a gas station, and it's twenty miles away. Jakob came prepared, though, with food galore and card games. Yes, card games, because we're teenage girls at a sleepover. Or maybe I'm being bitter because he's beaten me twelve times at Uno.

"Uno," he says, all proudly.

I glare. "You win. I quit."

He laughs. "You're such a sore loser. Come on!"

I change the color to yellow, and this guy puts down a yellow card. His last card, winning the game. Bullshit. I shake my head, throwing down the cards, but before I can complain, he takes me by my ankles and pulls me to him like I don't weigh anything. Once he has me in his lap, he kisses me ravishingly, and I fall into the kiss. I always do. He holds me by the back of my neck, his cock brushing against my center. When we aren't playing card games, we're playing with each other, and that part of the no distractions is really nice.

He tears his mouth from mine and sloppily kisses down my neck. He settles in the crook of my neck and runs his tongue along the hollow part. "Erik and I played all the time. That's how I'm so good. I used to let him win, though."

I lean into his head, cradling it as my eyes fall shut. "Can't let me win, huh?"

"No way. I gotta show off."

I snort. "You're such a pain." I inhale his scent, my body going lax against his. "Your brother is the same age as my sisters. We should hook them up."

He laughs. "Which one?"

"Probably Reese. Piper is too soft for someone like Erik."

He nods. "I wouldn't know. I've never met them."

I grin against his forehead. "Well played."

"I know," he says simply, kissing my neck. "I think this is the perfect time to ask if I can take you and your family out to dinner when we get back."

I move my lips along his brow as I tighten my legs around his waist and my arms around his neck. We're basically one big ball, and I refuse to move. "I know my mom would love that. She's been begging to meet you since Elli told her I was dating you."

I feel his lips curve. "Elli always has my back."

"Yes, it's annoying," I tease, and he laughs. "Speaking of, apparently dinner with her family did not go well for her and Shea. Her family, minus her dad and uncle, are real pieces of work. They treat Elli like she's basically a fat cow. It's annoying as shit. She's perfect."

Jakob kisses my neck. "Funny, I think you're perfect."

I nuzzle my nose into his hair. "I am far from perfect. You, of all people, should know that."

"How so?"

"I won't get where you are."

"You are where I am. See? You're in my arms."

He kisses up my jaw.

"You know what I mean."

"I do, and my position on the subject stands."

I exhale heavily. How is he so confident? So sure of us? I bite my lip as I thread my fingers through his hair. I didn't want to bring this up, but the more I think about it, the more I need to know. "Elli told me that Shea told her you've been in a lot of relationships."

"You talking about me?"

I set him with a pointed look. "She also said Shea told her you talk about me constantly."

He shrugs. "He isn't lying." He pulls back to look at me, a sly look on his face. "And yeah, I have been. I told you how many women I've been with—"

"No, I know, but I didn't realize those were all relationships. Did you love them?"

His eyes search mine. "To be honest, I thought I did love them. But I know, after meeting you, that wasn't true."

"How so?"

"It's different now."

Our eyes are locked as I ask, "What makes this different?"

"You," he says as simply as taking his next breath. "I swear to you, Harper, I'm not fucking with you when I say I saw you and I was done for. I know you just wanted sex. Hell, I knew that going in, but I didn't care. I knew this would be more. You gotta admit, that first time, something exploded between us."

I could admit it, but I won't. As I stare into his eyes, all these feelings start to suffocate me. I know when we get back, he has to leave again, and it's killing me to know he won't be in my arms like this. I know I should keep this light, but it actually stopped being light weeks ago.

"I think it was you who exploded."

He chuckles against my skin, setting me on fire. "Of course I did. You drive me crazy."

"That's been my plan all along."

His fingers glide up around my waist, dancing along my skin as he sucks on my neck. When he pulls back to look at me, I cup his cheek, and he leans into my hand. His eyes are dark and set on me, drinking me in. He's so damn handsome.

He has stubble dusting his jaw, and his hair is longer than it's ever been, falling into his gorgeous green eyes. I lean my head into his, and he cuddles me closer. "When we get back, I want you to meet my parents and Erik."

I kiss his nose. "Might as well have a huge dinner so we all can meet everyone."

"I'm down," he says without skipping a beat. "Name the time and place. We'll make it happen."

I grin. "You're serious."

"Like a heart attack."

"What if they don't like each other?"

He laughs. "Who cares? I like you, and you like me. So there." The certainty he has in us makes me confident. I want to be scared, but how can I when he's looking at me like this? Like the world is in the palm of our hands. He slides his nose against mine and along my top lip. "I found our song."

I eye him. "Our song?"

"Yeah, like how Shea and Elli have one."

I fight back my grin. "Is it good?"

"I think so," he says, and then he pulls out his phone. When he pushes play on the screen, I immediately recognize the song. Gavin DeGraw's "More than Anyone." I love this song. I've heard it so many times, and I even saw him in concert. It's a beautiful ballad, professing that he'll love her more than anyone else. As Gavin DeGraw sings with the soul only he could have, I rest my head against Jakob's shoulder. He holds me to him, running his hand up and down my back as the song plays. No one has ever given me a song and especially not one like this. I feel as if I'm on cloud nine. This one is special, super romantic, and I can't stop myself from loving it. I don't ever want to.

Man, all my emotions are firing like crazy right now. I feel so damn good.

I press my lips to his as his hands slide up my back, pulling my shirt up my body. When he pulls it off, he grins at me before capturing my lips once more. Since I'm not wearing a bra, he cups one of my breasts gently, squeezing it and loving my tit with his fingertips. When he trails his lips down my jaw to my neck, I lengthen my neck for him as he licks down my throat. I feel him growing underneath me as I lean back so he can nibble at my chest. He licks around my nipple before biting it gently. I cry softly, my whole body on fire as I arch into his mouth, needing more. He kisses the center of my chest and down lower before I use his shoulders to stand.

He watches as I push down my shorts, and he very quickly unfastens his jeans, releasing his cock. I hover over him and lower myself down onto him, and he fills me to the hilt. On my feet, I raise myself up and down on his cock, making him slip deeper and deeper as my ass slaps against his legs. He holds on to my waist, his head falling back as I quickly drop my pussy onto his cock. It's hitting all the right spots, and when I come, I shatter. I collapse onto him, needing the breather, but Jakob doesn't do breathers. He rolls us over, pushing my legs above my head before fucking every single breath out of my body. He pounds into me, each thrust deeper and harder than the last.

I can hardly breathe from how he must think I'm Gumby, but I don't dare complain. Each thrust sets off lights behind my eyes, and I'm thankful we're in the middle of nowhere. I'm screaming like he is breaking me, and to be honest, he just might be. I'm too far gone to even need to care. I want this. I crave this. All of him. I love it.

When he stills inside me, filling me, he lets out one hell of a moan before falling on top of me. My legs somehow move to his hips and wrap around him before I nuzzle my nose into his neck. I move my lips up his neck to his ear, cuddling deeper as I close my eyes, our heartbeats pounding together. As he wraps his arms around me, holding me so close that we may as well be one, I realize something.

I don't want him to ever let me go.

"Jakob."

He glides his lips along my cheek, kissing the side of my mouth. "Yeah, *kiska*?"

I sigh softly as our noses meet, and he stares into my soul. "I think I love you."

His face breaks into a wide grin, his eyes so soft, so full of promise. "*Kiska*, you don't think you love me. You do love me."

Now, I'm the one grinning. "How do you know?"

"Because I love you. Have loved you and will always love you. You really have no choice but to feel the same."

His mouth captures mine then, and my soul sings for him.

I think it always has, but I'm finally listening.

IN A RELATIONSHIP

JAKOB

"My mom is in love with you."

I laugh. "Of course she is," I chuckle as I head up the stairs of the hotel where we're staying. I was going to go out with the guys for lunch, but Shea is being a baby. He's all caught up on Elli and convinced she's going to meet someone else and leave him. For as much as he talks about her confidence being shitty, he should realize his is shitty too. That girl is in love with him; she isn't going anywhere. "How about your dad?"

"He's on the fence. He says you seem obsessed with me," she says in a teasing tone.

"And? Shouldn't he want me to be obsessed with you? Doesn't that mean I will die before I let anything happen to you?"

She sighs very loudly. "Stop. I love you. You don't have to keep wining and dining me."

I snort. "I'm not wining and dining you, Harper. I'm telling the woman I love that she means the world to me."

I hope she's smiling. I hope her face is that sweet color that drives me wild. "Well, I love you. Think of something gushy, and that's how I feel."

I laugh. "You gotta do something to make me believe it," I tease.

She barks out a laugh. "Like what? I gave you head all weekend. My TMJ is killing me. I mean, that alone should tell you I'm into you."

"Or you're into my cock."

"Well, duh," she laughs, and I chuckle. I took the stairs so I could talk to her before I got to the room. I know once I walk into the room, Shea is going to distract me, so I wanted to get in my time with Harper before she has to go shoot a wedding. She's always so busy but still makes time for me. Since our trip to the mountains, things have been amazing. When she said those three words I've been feeling for a while, I was breathless. Now I crave them. I love knowing how much she cares about me, and each day, she lets me know a little more. It's been really good.

I honestly didn't think she'd let me meet her parents, but she took me up on getting both our families together. Of course, our moms love each other. Our dads talked golf, while our siblings just sat there. I swear Piper has a thing for Erik, but Harper thinks he has something for Reese. Erik said it was neither; he's too focused on breaking into the NHL. He wants to play pro, and I don't blame him. When you get involved with a girl, she can take over your life. Harper has done that for me, and I don't know if Erik could handle the all-consuming love that Harper provides me with.

"What about your parents? Did they like me?"

"Harper, be real. My parents absolutely adored you. My dad says you're the one."

She takes in a sharp breath. "He said that?"

I laugh. "Yeah, *kiska*. He loved you. So did my mom, Erik

doesn't care one way or another, but he thought you were cool."

"Piper and Reese said I need to marry you."

"I wouldn't complain," I say, to which she groans.

"I'm just now admitting I love you. Relax there."

"Hey, we're one step closer."

She snorts. "You're insane."

"Yup, insanely in love with you."

"Jakey," she groans. "Stop. You make me feel all giggly."

"Good," I say, overwhelmed with all the feelings coursing through my body. "Listen, I gotta check on Shea. He's butthurt over Elli."

Harper laughs. "Why?"

"He thinks she's gonna cheat on him or something insane."

"What the hell?"

"Yeah, new relationship and all."

"I don't think that about you," she says simply. "I trust you."

"Exactly, because we're in love."

She groans more. "Bye, Jakob."

"Bye, *kiska*."

I hang up with the biggest grin on my face. When I reach the hotel room I share with Shea, I push the door open to find him sitting on the bed with his computer. He looks up at me and furrows his brows. "I thought you went out with the guys."

"Nah, thought you needed to talk."

Shea looks up, confused. "Huh?"

"You know, talk? Where your mouth moves and words come out," I say, falling onto my bed.

"Shut up, asshole. I know what talking is. I just don't know why I need to talk."

I shake my head, a small smile on my face. He's got it bad,

and it's cute. I like that he doesn't know how to handle what he is feeling. I think it's because it reminds me of Harper.

"Dude, you're moody as hell lately. I don't know what your problem is, but let it go. Did you and Elli get into a fight or something?"

"No, I just… I don't know."

He does know. He just needs a little push. "What's going on with you, dude? You don't call to go out anymore, and you are always with her. Is it really that serious?"

"Yeah, it is."

"Really?" I ask, curious as to how he is going to handle this.

"Things are different now, Jake. I'm not the guy I was six months ago."

I laugh loudly. "Well, no shit, Shea. I knew that, but are you seriously for real about her? I mean, we all know I'm for real about any girl I get involved with, but are you?"

He just nods. "I am. I love her."

There it is. With a grin filling my face, I say, "Good. You're getting older. You need to settle down."

He cringes, his whole body involved in the motion. "I never said anything about marriage, Jake."

I pull my computer out from under the bed. Figure I can play some games or look at some naked pictures of Harper. She sent me a few a while back, and when I miss her, which is basically all the time, I look at them. Makes me feel closer to her. "You didn't have to. You love her, so it will be just a matter of time. Since this is the one and only girl you have spent more than a day with."

Shea just shakes his head. "You sound like my mom."

"She's a smart woman," I remind him with a nod. I love Shea's mom. She's a hoot. But his dad, man, he is a blast. He's taken us fishing so many times, and he treats me like I'm his son. It's nice. I bet Harper would love them; they're just like my parents. A grin pulls at my lips. It's cute that she was worried if they liked her or not. They didn't stop talking to her and gushing over how gorgeous she is to her face. How else could they say they liked her?

She's so silly.

When my phone sounds, I look down to see a notification from Facebook.

Harper Allen says she's in a relationship with you.

I jump up, my computer going one way as I shout loudly.

"What the hell are you doing?" Shea yells back.

"I need my phone!"

He points to the TV, where I had set my phone right beside Shea's.

"Ah, thanks!" I yell, picking it up and calling Harper. I can hear it in her voice that she is about to be difficult.

Calmly, I say, "Hey there."

"Hey," she says cautiously.

"I saw your status."

"So? It means nothing!"

"Oh no, you don't. Don't deny it, baby girl. I saw it."

"Well, still. I just figure…may as well change it. You know, for the sake of everyone else and because we are in a…relationship, I guess. I mean, I love you."

I laugh hard. "I hate to say this, baby, but I told you so."

"Whatever. I gotta go," she says shortly, but I'm on cloud nine.

"Okay. Love you."

She sighs sweetly. "I love you more, Jakob."

As I hang up, I'm grinning from ear to ear.

I'm so winning at life right now.

With the puck on my stick, I move it back and forth as my team sets up. This game is an all-out war. We're fighting for the number one spot in our division, and with a win here, we'll make it. Apparently the Blues don't want to help us out and just lose. Nope, they want to be assholes and come at us like they're gonna get in first. They aren't even on anyone's radar. When Welch hits the ice, I rocket the puck to him and head toward the blue line. Shea is there, yelling, "Dump! Dump!"

Welch does as he's told before we all rush the net. Shea and I wait at the blue line as our forwards fight for the puck. When it comes to me, I send it to Shea for the one timer. He shoots, but it goes wide. I rush to it, getting there first and sending it to Welch, who is by the net. He shoots from his knees, but the goalie snaps it up like it's nothing. As we head to the bench, we're all frustrated. We've been fighting for a goal for the last ten minutes. They haven't even entered our zone, but their goalie decided to come to play today.

I reach for my Gatorade bottle, squirting some into my mouth as I watch the game. From beside me, Shea leans over the bench, yelling, "Guys! Tighten up. Fight! You got this. This is our game to lose!"

He isn't wrong. I draw in deep breaths as I watch our boys stay in their zone, not allowing them to leave. A minute passes before the goalie finally gets the puck, holding it to provide relief for his guys. Coach taps my shoulder, and I hop over the boards to go line up.

When Shea comes up beside me, I look over as he leans in. "One timer, left."

I nod. We've done this play before, and I'm stoked. Hopefully I can make the shot. Unfortunately, we don't win the face-off, and they carry it up the ice. I skate backward, watching the puck with laser focus. I read the play before the guy even has time to make it. He's trying to hit his forward.

Not on my watch.

I break the pass, getting it on my blade before I haul ass up the ice. What I don't see is their goon coming right for me. All I see is the world spinning before I hit the ice face first. I feel my teeth hit the back of my throat, pain explodes up my legs, and then everything goes black.

Completely black.

I blink a few times before I'm able to focus.

I feel like I'm flying, almost like I'm not even in my body. I feel pain, but it's numbed, if that makes sense. My damn face hurts like hell, though, and when I move my tongue along my gums, I realize my front teeth are gone. Fantastic. I'm sure that will turn Harper on real well. I roll my eyes in their sockets, trying to figure out if anything is broken in my face, but I don't feel anything. I move my fingers, but I can't feel if I'm moving my toes. That's not good. I sit up a bit to see my leg up in stirrups with a brace around it. Wow, this is awesome.

I then notice that someone is lying on my chest. I've seen this view many times before, and my heart soars.

She's here.

I move my hand to her head, threading my fingers in her hair, and she sits up quickly. Her eyes are bloodshot and drool is on her chin, but the stricken look on her face takes my breath away.

"Oh, Jakob," she cries before wrapping her arms around my neck as gently as she can. I hold her with one hand, kissing her jaw as she holds me close to her. "I was terrified."

"I'm sorry, *kiska*. I never saw that jackass coming," I say, and my voice sounds very fucked up. Groggy.

She kisses my neck, my jaw, my cheek, before pressing her lips hard against mine. "I thought I would never see you again. You hit the ice so awkwardly, it scared the hell out of me. I'm so sorry it took me so long to get here."

I make a face. "I just woke up. How long have you been here?"

"Um, about eight hours now. I got here when you were in

surgery," she says, holding me close, her nose still nuzzled in my neck. "I tried to get here before you went back, but Shea promised he would keep an eye on you."

"I don't remember any of this," I say, confused. "When did he leave?"

"When I got here. They had to fly out," she says, still not moving or letting me go. "Please don't ever do this to me again?"

I try to smile, but it sort of hurts. "Can't promise you that, my love. It's the name of the game."

"Ugh. I was worried you'd say that," she says, and I feel wetness then.

"*Kiska*, don't cry."

"I was so scared."

I kiss the side of her face. "It's all fine. I'm fine," I promise. "Do I look okay?"

She pulls back, such love on her face. "You're gorgeous."

I laugh. "I don't have teeth."

She waves me off. "Nope, they're gone. But you're a hockey player, so it's okay."

I give her a gummy grin. "Is my face broken?"

"Small hairline fracture on your nose, but your teeth took the brunt of the hit."

I nod before pointing to my leg. "What about that?"

"Torn MCL. The surgery was long."

I make a face, which stings a little. "How long am I out?"

She glares. "Who cares? You need to heal."

I shake my head. "Harper, how long?"

She looks broken as she whispers, "It's possible you won't play the rest of the season."

My heart sinks into my stomach as I shake my head. "Well, that's some shit."

She lays her head on my chest, and I tangle my fingers in her hair. "Don't worry. I truly believe you'll get back on the ice sooner rather than later. I'll work with you, go to everything. I got you."

I cup her face. "Thank you. But I'm not worried. I'm just hoping you still love me after a while."

She pulls in her brows. "Why wouldn't I?"

"I'm a huge baby when I'm hurting, and I'm sure I'll be annoying as hell."

Her lip wobbles as she reaches out, pinching my chin. "I don't care. I'm not leaving your side."

"No?"

She shakes her head. "Never."

She leans up, kissing my lips, and I hold her there. When she pulls back, I stare into her eyes. I'm convinced there is no woman I could ever love more. And while I want to believe her, I don't. She's a busy chick, and I'm sure she has better things to do than sit and nurse me back to health.

She proves me wrong, though, because she never leaves my side.

I stay at the hospital in St. Louis for several days before I am able to go back home. We've played more games of Uno than I thought she'd ever have the patience for. I even started letting her win. She worked while I slept, she entertained me, and she made sure to keep my parents updated every step of the way. Harper was a godsend and, honestly, my saving grace. There were many times I wanted to give up because the pain was too much, but she wouldn't let me. She was patient, she was encouraging, and I didn't think I could love her more than I already did.

Bryan Fisher, Elli's uncle and the owner of the team, sent his plane to bring me home, so it will be a nice ride back to Nashville. I'm pretty sure Harper pulled those strings, since Bryan doesn't do that for anyone else. I am already comfortable, but I let Harper fuss over me and make sure I'm settled. When she sits beside me, she pulls out her phone and sends a few texts. I assume they are to my mom, hers, and Elli.

"I wish I could text."

She looks over at me. "Do you need your phone?"

"No. I can't text, remember? Bad English."

She smiles. "Well, we're about to have a lot of downtime. I'll teach you."

I reach over, taking her hand to keep her from texting. She looks back at me, a small smile on her face as she threads her fingers through mine. "I'm texting your mom and dad that we're on our way home."

"I know, but I gotta tell you something," I say, bringing her hand to my lips. "I love you, Harper Allen."

She beams over at me. "I love you."

I kiss her hand once more. "I want us to move in together."

She nods. "I figured I'd just come to you since it would—"

"No, I want us to find a place together. Our home."

Her lips part a little as her eyes search mine. "Our home?"

"Yes, ours. I want to plant our roots, *kiska*. I love you, and if these last few weeks proved anything, it's that I don't want to be apart from you unless I have to be."

Her eyes start to water a bit, and she nods slowly. "I want the same thing. It only took you tearing your MCL and losing your teeth for me to realize I never want to be apart from you, Jakob."

I pull her to me, and her mouth is right there for the taking. "I'd go through all the pain over again and again just to hear you say those words."

She kisses my top lip. "I love you, Jakob."

"Oh, *kiska*, I love you more than I could ever imagine."

WE'RE DOING THIS TOGETHER

HARPER

"Elli?"

I yank my keys out of her door as Adler, her fat as fuck pug, comes running for me. The word *running* is used lightly. He thinks he's fast, and Elli feeds into his confidence. Those two are two peas in a pod. One would think Shea would speak the truth, but I feel he's feeding into Adler's false sense of security too.

"Elli?" I call out once more as I set down her mail. We went out the other night, and I get it, we're getting older. But it isn't good when you're still in bed three days after the drunken night. I'm worried it's worse than Elli lets on. She told me to leave the soup and new meds at the door, not to check on her, but I could hear in her voice she wasn't good. I head down the hall, and I hear her moaning something along the lines of "Go away," but I don't pay her any mind. I've been dealing with a wounded bear of my own. I knew I loved Jakob, but if his injury taught me anything, it was that I *really* love him. Like, with my whole heart.

That asshole.

Lord, he complains about everything. He is never comfortable. I'll give it to him, it's hard to get around on one leg looking like a damn pirate, but when he acts like a hard-ass in front of Shea or his buddies, I don't want to hear that shit. He's been a thorn in my side. But it's funny... I don't trust anyone else to care for him. It was a shock to me too; I never saw this coming. This all-consuming love. Alas, Jakob's got me locked in.

When I round the corner into her bedroom, I find her, facedown, with her hair everywhere. I can tell by the color of her skin that she isn't good. "Elli?"

I go to her side, but through her hair, she says, "Harper, I told you to leave everything at the front. I'm fine."

"You don't look fine," I point out, noticing all the Gatorade bottles and the trash can that has vomit in and around it. I tuck my phone into my back pocket before setting her soup on the nightstand along with one of her meds. The others weren't ready. "Same as always? Everything hurts?"

"Everything," she groans, covering her face with her blanket. "Just go."

"Let me help you shower."

"No, I'm fine."

I look around at her room, the condition she's in, and my body vibrates with anger. "Elli, how long has this been going on?"

"Just two days, I promise."

"Where is Shea?"

Even with the blanket covering her face, I can see her brow furrow. "I don't know. I haven't talked with him on the phone, just texts. Why?"

"He should be here taking care of you."

Still with a face full of confusion, she drawls out, "Why? I'm fine."

"You're not fine. You're having an episode. Does he even know this is happening?"

She doesn't answer me as I reach down to get the trash bin. I'm almost to the bathroom when she says, "Just go. I'm fine."

"Damn it, Elli! If you tell me you're fine one more *time*, I'm gonna kick your ass. You're not fine. You need someone to sit with you. I didn't even realize it was this bad." I clean out the trash can in the tub and put a new bag in it before heading back into her room. "I mean, I don't even like people, and I would want someone to help me puke in the right place. Is this even gonna come out of the carpet?"

It doesn't look like it will to me, but it doesn't seem like Elli gives a shit. "Who cares? Leave me here to die."

Yup, she's sick. "No, Elli. Seriously, either you call Shea, or I do."

She actually sits up, and I can tell it make her nauseated by the way she clutches her blanket. She takes in a deep breath, and my heart aches at the sight. Her skin is a nasty white, and she has dark circles around her eyes. This isn't the first time, nor will it be the last, and still, it kills me. Very sternly, she says, "He cannot see me like this. He will dump me on sight."

I squint at her, unsure what I am hearing. "Are you insane? You're sick—and not even with a communicable disease. I know the dude, and I doubt he would do that. He's gonna be madder you didn't tell him the truth."

"I can't let him see me like this," she says adamantly.

"Elli, if he can't see you like this, then when can he? When it's time to move in together, he's gonna see it. What are you going to do? Hide?"

She falls back into her pillows, obviously weak. "No. I don't know. Just go."

I shake my head. "I would beat Jakob's ass if he didn't call me and he was sick like this. You're gonna piss off Shea. Believe me on that."

"He can't see this. I'm disgusting."

"And he won't care! He loves you! All of you—even the stubborn part that doesn't think she's good enough."

My chest actually hurts that she doesn't seem to understand that. Did her ex really fuck her up that bad? I mean, let's be honest, my many exes did, and I'm just now opening up to Jakob. Mainly because he wouldn't leave me the hell alone.

Hmm. Idea.

"Just leave me alone. I don't want him seeing this," she moans, moving her hand up and down her body. Even that seems to hurt her.

"Did you at least tell him you were sick? Like, really sick, or are you telling him the same lie you told Bryan and your dad? That it's just a cold? And by the way, I didn't rat you out to them."

I expected some gratitude. But nope. "Harper," she says sternly. "It doesn't matter. I'm fine. It will pass."

"You need supervision!"

"I am a grown-ass woman. I don't need supervision. I can handle this."

I glare. "Elli, you're puking so much, you're missing the trash can!"

"I'm fine! Go."

She covers her head, and I shake my own. "Whatever. Not all your meds were ready, but I brought your soup."

"Thank you. I'll go get the other meds later."

I make a face. "Don't you need them to get better?"

She groans. "I'll figure it out since asking you is out of the question now."

"Wow, you're a real asshole," I say as I head out of the room. I know she doesn't mean to be rude; I know she doesn't feel well and is lashing out at me because it's easy. It doesn't make it right, but I know she doesn't mean it. I go to the kitchen to feed Adler, and while I fill his bowl, I pull out my phone. I dial Shea's number, and when he answers, I glare at the picture of Elli and me that hangs on her fridge. She's lucky I love her ass for life.

"What the hell, Shea Adler!"

He's taken aback. "Harper?"

I fill the water dish as I say, "The one and only. Listen here, buddy. Why is it that I am taking care of your best friend, but you can't take care of mine?"

"What? What are you talking about?" he asks, genuinely confused, and for good reason. I'm sure she hasn't told him shit.

"Elli. I can't do both and work. You're going to have to take one of them."

"Wait, Harper. What's wrong with Elli?"

Figures. I can't believe her. "What? You haven't talked to her? Oh God, please don't tell me you don't know she's sick."

"I knew she was sick, but she told me she just needed a few days to herself to sleep and heal. What the hell is wrong?"

"Ugh, damn it. Why does she do this? She lied to her dad, her uncle, and now you. Wonderful."

I can hear the frustration in his voice, but he's trying to stay calm. "Harper, what the hell is wrong with Elli?"

"She's sick. It happens every once in a while," I say slowly. "She starts to feel run-down, and then she's just out for a couple days. She had to change her meds this time, so it must have been bad when it happened. She called me to bring her soup and to pick up her meds. I got mad because that's what you should be doing since you are her boyfriend."

"You're right. I should be doing that…if I actually knew she was that sick!"

"Well, now you know. Her meds are at Walgreens, and she

likes the chicken noodle from Panera. Holler if you need anything else. Do you have a key?"

"No."

Are they even in a relationship? Not only does Jakob have my key and I have his, we are looking for a place of our own. I know Shea and Elli might not be where Jakob and I are, and I can't compare them to us, but I wouldn't hide something like this from him. Shea is about to get a rude awakening, and fuck if I don't hope he steps up. He better step up and make her feel special, or I'll take him out. "Well, stop by the studio and get it, because she won't be able to unlock the door. She's really weak."

I say bye and then hang up before I start to clean up just a bit. It's a wreck, but to be honest, I want Shea to see it. I want him to know what he is getting into because this isn't something that will go away. Her thyroid disease is no joke. As I head out of the kitchen, I dial Jakob's number on FaceTime.

He answers on the second ring as I walk out the front door. "Hey, baby. Sorry, I was in the bathroom. Is Elli okay?"

My heart warms. He's just a good dude. Elli isn't even his friend, and he cares for her. "She's pretty bad off. I called Shea."

"Good. He'll take good care of her. I'm glad you didn't listen to her and went over."

"Yeah. I knew she wasn't okay. It just irritates the hell out of me that she thinks it's okay to sit over here and suffer."

"Why didn't she call Shea?"

"She doesn't want him seeing her like this."

He scoffs. "Does she not know that's gonna piss him off?"

"Who knows. She's so worried he's gonna dump her. Everything about her is wonderful. It's her insecurities that will ruin everything."

"True that," he says softly. "Plus, doesn't she know it's all the little things, the things you don't even suspect are special, that make you special?"

I grin. "You think that about me?"

"Yeah, I do," he says softly. "I didn't know I would love your bad breath in the morning or miss it."

I laugh from my belly. "That's your bad breath!"

His eyes are dark as he holds my gaze, ignoring my laughter. "No, *kiska*, that's you. I thought mine was bad, but then I woke up beside you."

I almost fall over myself laughing. "Shut up. You're so mean!" He just laughs as I open my car door. "You sure Shea will care for her?"

"Harp, he loves her. A lot. He'll take damn good care of her."

I nod as I get into my car. "I'm so mad at her. She looked like utter shit, and the whole time, all I could think was if you did this to me, hid it from me, I'd kick your ass."

He laughs. "Bring it," he teases, and I grin. "But I wouldn't do that, and you better not do it to me."

"Never."

"Good. Plus, let's be honest. Look at us. You're my own private nurse, basically. Bandages, braces, and blow jobs. It's really great."

I snort. "You're impossible," I say as I look back at Elli's house. A part of me wants to go back in there and care for her myself, but I feel strongly that Shea should do it. If I'm gonna trust him to love and care for Elli for the rest of her life, he has to see this. She would hide it until the day she dies if she could. It makes me sad. She's so wonderful, so perfect. I hate that she doesn't think so. If I could take out her ex, I would. Get a professional hit man. I'd do it.

"You on your way here?"

"Yeah," I say as I turn off her road. "I'll be about an hour, depending on traffic."

"Sounds good. See you in a bit."

"Love you."

"Love you more, *kiska*."

As we hang up and I move my phone from the holder on the dash into the seat beside me, I know he means it.

I just hope Shea means it about Elli.

I learned a couple weeks later that he did, in fact, love her like I assumed.

I suspect, more than he loves himself.

Not only did Shea step in and take care of Elli, she said she fell even more hopelessly in love with him. He came in and did exactly what I hoped he would. He was her partner. He cared for her, cleaned up, and made her feel better. Apparently hockey isn't the only talent he has. Shea Adler can sing —and pretty damn well from what I'm told. I was shocked, but as I stand here in the middle of the Belmont Mansion and watch as he skillfully moves across the dance floor with my best friend, I realize Shea is a man of many talents.

One being making my best friend deliriously happy.

When he came to me with the idea for Elli's birthday, a *Pride and Prejudice*-themed bash, complete with period costumes, a violin quartet, and all her favorite foods, I knew he was the one. I don't care if Elli doesn't even know—I do. They will get married, they will have tons of babies, and they will be so happy, it will disgust me. Even with me having my own Darcy, I have to give props where props are due. And they're due to the guy standing in the middle of the floor, in full costume with a pair of Chucks on, whom Elli can't stop beaming at.

It's quite the show.

Jakob wraps his arms around my waist before his lips come to my jaw. He dressed up, but he wouldn't put on the period socks. With his brace, it would be hard anyway. I offered to try, though. But he doesn't need them. He looks stunning in his red velvet costume with a frilly little tie. He left his hair wild, unkempt, and I'm really digging it. He somehow got them to allow him to wear his Converse. Really, I don't care. I'm just glad he's up, out of the house, and with me. He kisses my jaw once more, and I lean into him as I smile. "She looks so beautiful."

He hugs me, watching our best friends. "I think they look really happy."

I turn my face so my mouth touches the side of his. "We are too."

Jakob chuckles, nodding. "We were happy before them," he says with a kiss. "When you finally gave in to me."

I lean my nose into his cheek. I don't know if it's the place, the ambiance, or what, but I'm feeling such strong emotions. Overpoweringly in love. "I'm sorry I made you work so hard for me."

He kisses my cheek. "Best thing I ever worked for."

I grin. "Even better than the NHL?"

"Way better. This is life, *kiska*. Life."

Man, he makes it really hard to breathe. "I love you, Jakob."

"I love you, my love," he says with a wink, and when he brings me in closer, I lean into him. I rise up on my toes, ready to kiss him, but he doesn't meet me. "So, I went to your car to get my night meds I had asked you to bring me, and I saw the bag on the passenger seat. Actually, it was the Skittles I saw. And you know…Skittles."

In that instant, everything stops. I know why I've been feeling a certain way all day. Actually, it's been more than a few days, but I sure as hell wasn't ready to face it. Or discuss it with Jakob yet.

"I saw the test."

I swallow hard, leaning into him to hide my face. "Yeah."

"You think so?"

I press my lips together as I snuggle my nose into his neck. "I'm eight days late."

"That's over a week," he says slowly, and I feel his heart rate pick up in speed. "So, more than likely, you are?"

I swallow hard. "I don't know," I say breathlessly. I refuse to cry. Why cry? We're the ones who were banging without condoms. We're the ones who weren't careful and never even seemed to think of the repercussions. Nope, we were just having sex with no cares whatsoever. Well, we had cares—getting off—but no concerns about what could happen.

I feel his hand in mine before I realize he is pulling me out of the room. There are people everywhere—Elli has the biggest family imaginable, and even my family is here. He somehow dodges everyone, and when we start up the stairs, I find myself asking a question I already know the answer to. "Where are we going?"

"To the bathroom," he says, and then he pulls the test out of his pocket. "It's test time."

My stomach drops. "Now?"

"Now. Right now."

And for the first time, I can't read him. Is he happy? Scared? Mad? I don't know. I do know that I'm a lot terrified and unsure what is about to happen. We go into a room, opening the door with a keycard he apparently had. "I got this for us."

I would usually be all excited and thinking how sweet he is, but that test in his hand is taunting me. He locks the door behind us, and I take the test from him. "I'll be back—"

"Ha. Nope. We're doing this together."

He takes the test and starts to open it as I walk into the bathroom. I pull up the skirt of my costume as he hands me the stick for me to pee on. I sit on the toilet and look up at him as I pee. "Wow, a glimpse into our future."

He laughs. "It'll be the best part of my day. Watching you pee."

"Well, if it is positive, we'll be teaching someone else to pee in a toilet."

"Again," he says, stealing my attention, "it'll be the best part of my day."

A warm feeling burns throughout me as I put the stick on the sink and wipe. When I stand, he comes over to me, wrapping his arms around my waist and putting his head on my shoulder as I wash my hands. I'm pretty sure the test showed positive before I even set the stick down. I just tried to ignore it. I feel his intake of breath when he realizes what we're looking at. Tears flood my eyes, and I close them tight.

"Are you happy?" he asks, and I find myself smiling.

"I am."

"Good, because I am too, *kiska*. Honestly. I couldn't ask for anything better," he says, and then he turns me in his arms, kissing me hard on the lips. I'm terrified, but I feel safe in his embrace. With him. As we kiss, my body is vibrating with energy. I really don't know how I got here.

But hell if I'm not thankful this is where I am.

FOR REAL? FOR REAL.

JAKOB

I lie between Harper's legs, my head on her pelvic bone as I run my fingers along her stomach while she's on the phone. She doesn't have a bump, and no one knows or even suspects she's pregnant, but I know. I know my baby is growing inside the love of my life. Talk about punching you in the stomach and it feeling damn good. I swear she is glowing, and every single fiber of my being is in love with her. I just want to stare at her and tell her how gorgeous I think she is. I know she is nervous, that she is scared, even, but I've got her. I've got her the way she had me when I got hurt.

She's my favorite team member.

I move my finger in circles as I watch her talk. "I told you we were looking. Just because you have commitment issues doesn't mean I do," she says to Elli. I guess it's hard for Elli to wrap her mind around the fact that we're buying a house together. Unlike her, and probably Harper, I knew from the jump that this would happen. I didn't plan the baby this soon —I thought maybe we'd have some years just us two—but this is a surprise I wanted. I was hoping we would be married and all that jazz first just so our parents wouldn't be disappointed, but I don't care. Nothing and no one can take this joy from me.

I have it all.

"Great. I'll text you the address."

She hangs up and looks down at me as she types something quickly. "She's being difficult and acting as if just because she doesn't want to commit, that I can't. I mean, I get it. I was very resistant, but then I almost lost you—"

"I tore my MCL. Hardly almost lost me," I say dryly. "Won't be the last time either."

She visibly ignores that comment and says, "It felt like I was losing you when I couldn't speak to you. And like I said, that woke me up. I refuse to live without you."

I cup her waist in my hands. "Right back atcha."

"Especially now that you've knocked me up."

I chuckle. "You weren't going anywhere before that either."

She shrugs. "Probably not." She exhales heavily as she closes her eyes, and I watch her. I don't know what it is, but I feel like I'm seeing her for the first time. Like she's brand-new and all mine. "I feel you staring at me."

"Well, you're so beautiful."

She winces. "I'm pretty sure I still have puke in my hair."

"You don't."

She opens her eyes and takes a deep breath. She reaches up, cupping my face. "We need to get ready."

"In a few," I say softly, leaning into her hand. "Are we telling Shea and Elli today?"

She doesn't even hesitate. "No. Not yet."

I bring in my brows. "Why not?"

"I want to wait to tell people," she says slowly, her eyes searching mine.

"Why? Do you want to be married first?"

"No. That's not it at all," she says, waving me off. "I wouldn't ask that of you. It's fine."

"Do you want to get married?"

"Are you asking?"

I grin. "I might be."

She shakes her head. "I want you to ask me because you want me."

"Well, that—"

"Jakob, not now," she says softly, her eyes holding mine. "I'm just worried is all."

"Worried?"

Now she hesitates, her eyes locking with mine. "I lost two babies before."

I narrow my eyes. "With who? And why didn't you tell me this?" I sit up, getting on my knees. "I thought you didn't have relationships."

She sits up too, holding up her palms to me. "I didn't. I really didn't."

"But you were with someone to have a baby?"

She gives me a look. "We both know I was not a saint before you, Jakob. Come on."

My eyes burn into hers. "When?"

"I got pregnant in high school, but I lost it almost immediately. At the time, it was for the best since I wasn't ready. Plus, the guy cheated on me a couple days later, so that was awesome."

What a dick, but I'm still annoyed I'm just learning of this. We've been together a while, and she never mentioned anything.

"Then I got pregnant again a couple years ago, and when I told the guy, he left me. And right when I decided to do it on my own, I lost the baby."

"I wouldn't leave you."

She cups my neck, holding me close. "Oh, I know, Jakob. I know that."

"Okay, but why didn't you tell me before now?"

She looks away, pulling up her shoulders. "I don't know. We've never spoken about kids, and I don't like talking about it."

"But it's me," I say. My feelings are hurt. "I've told you everything."

"I know, and I'm sorry I didn't tell you. I think it's because I thought I couldn't have kids and you'd leave me."

I just stare at her, my gaze holding hers. "Harper, I'm not going anywhere. With or without kids, you're mine." When her eyes start to well up, my stomach clenches. "You know that."

"I think I do, but sometimes I don't think I believe it."

"Well, start," I insist, kissing her palm. "So, when can we tell everyone?"

She looks away once more, her face filling with apprehension. "I don't want to tell anyone until I'm four months."

I just look at her. I'm supposed to keep this secret that long?

"You're not going to tell Elli for three months that you're pregnant?"

She nods. "Both times, I told Elli and my sisters, and I lost it. I want to wait. I want to make sure it sticks, that you stick."

I can't be mad at her. I want to be, I want to hate that she didn't tell me about the past pregnancies, but I won't. I'm not surprised. She's questioned this, us, since the beginning. She was so reluctant to commit to me, and after all this, I understand why. When shit got rough, people left. That won't happen with me. I'm in this for the long haul. The till death do us part shit. "You stood beside me through the roughest injury of my life, *kiska*, and nursed me back. They thought I wouldn't play the rest of the season, but look who's playing next week."

She wraps her arms loosely around my neck. "That's all you, Jakob. You're a beast."

"Because of you. Because of your love, and Harper, I swear I fell in love with you all over again."

Her eyes light up. "I love you, Jakob. I do."

As I gaze into her eyes, I'm lost, and I don't want anyone but her to find me. "I had hoped to be the one to support and love you through every hard thing known to man, but now… Now, it's not a hope—it's going to happen. It's a promise."

"It is?"

"Yup, it's me and you, forever. We'll sprinkle in some kids here and there."

She sits up, leaning her face into mine. "I love that."

"Good," I say, kissing her lips. "Now, get up, let's go meet our friends, and maybe us being so in love and moving forward will push them in the same direction."

She laughs. "They need a lot of pushing."

I watch as she gets up, drinking in the beauty that is my future. I can't wait until she is showing. She's already so beautiful, but with my baby inside her, on display, it will up that beauty by a million. "Hey, Harp."

She looks over her shoulder at me as she slides a pair of jeans up those gorgeous thighs. "Yeah?"

"You'll never be alone."

Her eyes soften as she nods. "Right back atcha."

I grin and exhale. "And I wanted to marry you before the baby because I love you. Only you. And this baby… It's one hell of a bonus."

The most gorgeous and stunning grin covers that sweet face of hers. She walks over to me and falls into my lap as I wrap my arms around her, kissing her hard on the lips. As we fall onto the bed, I know we'll be late to see Shea and Elli. But being underneath Harper, her sweet lips on mine and all the love in the world coursing through my body, I find it hard to muster up any feelings of guilt.

Not when I feel like I'm winning all eighty-two regular season games.

Not when I feel like I scored all the winning goals.

And definitely not when I feel she is the ultimate prize, better than the Stanley Cup.

The next six weeks were crazy eventful.

Once it was time for me to hit the ice with my team, I only got to play one game with Shea before he got hurt. It was a straight bullshit hit, but it's the name of the game. Our bodies aren't made of metal, unfortunately. I worried he wouldn't be back, but like me, he doesn't give up. So, while I was finding my footing and also buying a house, Shea was healing and doing a great job of it, because he has come back sooner than expected.

Which is good for us. We have to have our captain.

Shea's presence is needed on the ice; he runs shit, and we all look to him. As I sit beside him, putting on my gear, I tell him about the house and how his sister, Grace, is working her ass off to make it perfect. I've respected Harper's wishes and not told anyone about the baby, but it's killing me. I want to scream it from the rooftop. I want to wear a shirt that says: *I knocked up the hottest woman in the world*, but I can't. She said a hard no on the shirt idea. Sometimes, I wonder if she even loves me. I kid. I know for a fact she does.

Things are fantastic.

"Harper is insane if she thinks I want a gray house."

Shea jeers as he puts on his chest pad. "Gray is the new white, from what Grace is saying."

"Great, now you're on their side," I grumble, and he laughs. "How's the looking going?"

He scrunches up his face. "Elli is driving me up the fucking wall. She has this list of shit she needs, and I'm trying really hard to respect it, but it's like nothing is good enough for her. I've loved like eight houses, but they don't have everything she needs."

"Why don't you just build a house?"

He gives me a look. "I offered that, and she said no. She wants a house with bones that have memories or something like that. Pretty sure she got it out of a country song."

I snort. "You'll find it."

"Yeah," he says slowly. "I think I'm gonna ask her to marry me."

"Do it," I encourage. "Go see Harper's sister, Piper. She set me up real nice."

His eyebrows shoot up. "You already bought a ring?"

"Yeah," I say happily. "I don't know when I'm asking. I'm waiting for the right moment, but the ring, it's perfection, totally Harper. Piper knows Elli. She'll help you out."

"Where?"

"Tiffany's. Ask for Piper." Shea nods before he laces up his skates while I make sure my elbow pad is in place. "Ready?"

A grin takes over his face, which I'm thankful for. He's been a bit down with the injury and the frustrations with Elli. "More than ready."

I stand, hopping on my skates. "Good. Let's do this."

He stands beside me, and we bump fists. "Hell yeah."

I want to bash my head into the wall.

Grace, Shea's sister and our interior designer, stands before us by the bar in the kitchen with paint samples, textiles, and more home shit that I really don't care about. Harper won't move in until the house is done. I was cool with it before, but now, I just want to live in our house. I hate her apartment. It's so small, and I want a dog. I'm just ready to keep the ball moving, and I feel like dealing with all the house stuff is stalling us. Our conversations are only about the house or work and maybe sometimes the baby if she's puking her brains out. She's been really sick lately, and I hate it for her because she won't stop. She is headstrong and works her ass off, and then she comes to the house to make decisions.

I swear, I'll never love anyone more.

"What do you think, Jakob?" Harper asks, and I shrug.

"To be honest, I don't care," I say, and by the way she and Grace are looking at me, I'm realizing that's not the answer they wanted. "I don't even know why we're replacing the stairs or the railing. I like them."

"I want it to go with the rest of the house," Harper says, shooting me a pointed look. "You said I can do what I want."

"I know, but I want to move in," I say, holding her gaze. "I want to live here with you, and no offense, Grace, but I want to paint and shit like that."

"When, Jakob? You're gone all the time, and I'm working. This is the best thing for us."

She's not wrong, but I still want to do it myself. This is a losing battle, and I'm over it. "Fine. Get what you want."

I walk off, heading into our grand living room. It's got high ceilings and a massive fireplace that I plan on doing Harper in front of. We just have to move in first. I look over to the stairs, and they're fine to me. I don't know why she wants to replace them. I don't realize Harper has come into the room until her hand slides up my back. I look down at her, turning and wrapping my arm around her waist. "I'm sorry. I'm just ready to make this our home."

"It's okay," she says, kissing my shoulder.

"I know I'm a pain."

She shrugs. "I take your good days with your bad."

I glance down at her, kissing her forehead.

"They're gonna redo the stairs and paint the bedrooms except for the baby's room. I want to do that with you."

My lips quirk. "I want that too."

"Hopefully blue," she says softly. "A sweet little hockey room."

I shake my head. "No, a pink princess room. With glitter and all that shit. Something to drive you wild because she'll be the opposite of you."

She beams up at me. "And hopefully everything like you."

Fuck, I love this woman. "As long as she has your eyes."

"No! Your eyes are so much better."

"Maybe a mix."

"A mix would be good," she gushes, and then she kisses my shoulder. "We're really doing this."

I mock. "*Kiska*, we've been doing this for a while."

She exhales lightly. "We can move in next week."

My heart skips a beat. "Really?"

"Really," she says softly, leaning into me. "I want to move in too. I hate my apartment."

I sigh dramatically. "Me too!"

She laughs as she wraps her arms around me.

"I'm ready to start our lives here."

"Agreed," she says, and I lean my head to hers as we look out the windows into the huge backyard. We plan to put a massive swing set back there. When I was growing up, that was all I wanted. Somewhere to play. And now that I have the chance to give that to my child and play with them, I'm stoked. I kiss Harper's temple as our future plays out in my head.

I can't wait.

"Shea and Elli found a place."

"Good," I say as my grin grows. "I know he was stressing."

"Yeah, she was too. Driving me nuts."

I chuckle softly. "You know he told me he's thinking of asking her to marry him."

Harper's eyes widen as she looks up at me. "No way!"

"Yeah, I sent him to Piper."

She points to me. "Good looking out. My sister is broke. That's going to be a great commission."

I laugh. "I think she's doing just fine after the ring she sold me."

Gone is the grin, and soon, her eyes widen. "I'm sorry, what?"

Her grin may be gone, but mine is just widening more. "She sold me a pretty badass ring. It's huge."

Harper just blinks.

"Wanna see it?"

"For real?"

I feel tears burning my eyes. I've been waiting for this moment, and to be honest, I didn't realize this was it. I thought we'd be at a dinner or on a beach or something. I don't know. Yet here we are. With emotion clogging in my throat, I say, "For real."

Harper watches as I reach into my pocket, pulling out my wallet. I open the change section and take out the ring I've been carrying around, waiting for the right time to pull it out and ask this woman to be mine for the rest of my life. Her eyes fill with tears at the sight of the 2.5-carat round diamond that sits exceptionally well on a diamond-studded gold band.

She covers her mouth, but the sob still escapes. "Oh, Jakob."

I let her go, slowly lowering to the floor on one knee. "Harper," I start, but then the emotion takes over. "I fucking love you. I love all of you, and I want to make a life with you. I want to raise kids with you, I want to make this house a home with you, I want to grow old with you, and then I want to die beside you. Marry me, Harper. Please make all those hopes and dreams reality."

She only nods before she throws herself into me, wrapping her arms around my neck. I fall back from the force of her embrace, holding her close as our lips meet. Her little bump presses into my gut, and love explodes inside me. We are doing it. We are living the life we are making.

When she pulls back, her eyes sparkling with tears and adoration, I hold her tighter. "Tomorrow."

I furrow my brow. "Huh?"

"Tomorrow. I wanna get married tomorrow."

I laugh. "For real?"

She smiles, her eyes bright. "For real! Something small, just us and Shea and Elli. I don't want a huge to-do. I just want us."

My body vibrates with excitement. "Yes. Fuck yes."

She squeals as our lips meet once more—and once more, I feel as if I have fallen in love with her all over again.

If this is how it's gonna be the rest of my life, I am about to be one happy dude.

WE WON'T BREAK UP, WILL WE?

HARPER

As I lie against Jakob's ribs, he moves his fingers through my hair while I hold my hand up, admiring my gorgeous ring. He picked the most classic, most breathtaking ring I have ever seen in my life. I'd never thought about what I wanted my ring to look like, but this right here, this is it. While I lie here, I can't believe this is where I am. I was so resistant to starting something with him. I always felt he cared more for me than I did him, but that's not the case anymore. I think everything changed when he got hurt. That was the turning point in our relationship. The moment I realized I couldn't live without him.

I stroke my hand over my growing belly and sigh softly. When Jakob's hand covers mine, I smile as I turn my head to look at him. His eyes are closed, and he looks so peaceful. Things are progressing so wonderfully for us. The movers are coming at the end of the week, and we'll be moved in before he leaves for his next week-long trip. The Assassins are making a huge push for the play-offs. They're in third right now, and they really want to end in first so they'll play the last seed and then have home-ice advantage. I laugh at myself in surprise; I'm shocked by my hockey knowledge, but it comes with the player. Jakob has made sure I know everything, and I don't resist him. I let it happen because I care. I care about his job—and about him.

Crazy how things change.

What's really crazy is that when he gets back, he'll come home to our home. We'll find out what we're having soon, and then it will be baby room time. I was terrified early in the pregnancy, but I feel so great now. I feel the baby is secure inside me and not going anywhere. I never was able to fall in love with my baby before, but now, I am so totally and helplessly in love with it that the thought of losing it nearly ruins me. Jakob, being the wonderful man he is, won't let me. He's too damn positive, and I'm so thankful for that.

I can't help but smile. This life, all this, is what I thought I never wanted, but then he came along.

He turned my world upside down.

Jakob slides his hand along my jaw, cupping my chin before running his thumb over my lip. "Did you call Elli?"

"Not yet. I am waiting for the minister to get back to me."

He lies there, a serene look on his gorgeous face as I gaze at him. "I tried calling Shea, but he isn't answering."

"That's odd. Usually he answers, huh?"

"Yeah," he says, but he doesn't seem very worried. "So, we're thinking tomorrow?"

"I think so, depending on the minister's schedule."

"Cool." He slips his fingers into my hair. "And we're sure we don't want our parents there?"

I smile. "Do you want your mom and dad?"

He opens his eyes then, and he looks sheepish as he says, "I kinda do."

I smile. I love this man. "Okay, we'll plan for Friday morning, so it gives everyone time to come."

He leans up, kissing me on the lips. "Thank you."

I kiss him back, and he grins against my mouth. When he lies back, he exhales and says, "I feel we should name the boy Jakob Junior."

I scowl. "No way. I hate Juniors."

"What? Why?"

"I don't know," I say, dialing Elli's number. It goes straight to voice mail. Weird. "I mean, he has your last name, and he'll carry that on. Why do we need to give him your first name?"

He shrugs. "Fine, then something Russian."

I nod. "I can go with that." I dial Elli's number once more, thinking maybe the first time was a fluke. "I want Allison for a girl, though."

"Allison?" he asks. This time, it does ring, but then it goes to voice mail. Again, weird.

"Yeah, Ally for short," I say, typing out a message to Elli.

"Why?"

I grin. "When Elli and I were younger and had our baby dolls, mine was always Ally and hers was always Posey. It reminds me of that friendship, and I want to honor that. You can pick the middle name, though," I say with a wink, and he laughs.

"That's sweet. Special, even. I'm good with it."

I beam. "You're the best," I say, and finally, Elli answers.

"Harper, not right now."

Oh no, something is wrong. I sit up quickly, holding my stomach as I ask, "Are you okay? You sound bad. Do you need me—"

"No, I'm—" She pauses as a sob escapes her. "I saw Shea and Victoria kissing."

My eyes widen, and I actually gasp. "No way." Shea? Kiss Elli's sister, Victoria? I mean, she is gorgeous, model-skinny and all that, but I thought Shea was better than that. I thought he loved Elli. Surely this is a joke. "Are you sure?"

"Yes! I saw them, Harper!"

My stomach drops. I can't believe it. For a solid five minutes, she sobs. She can't speak, and I don't ask her to. I just listen to her cry, slowly but surely breaking my heart.

"Can I come over?"

"No, I'm a mess."

"I don't care," I say, getting up and putting my shoes on. "I'm coming."

"No. Please, just let me be. I need to breathe. I need to cry, and I don't want anyone here for that."

I bite my lip. "Elli, I can bring over candy and food. We can binge and talk shit."

Another round of sobs. "I can't. Not right now. I need to be alone."

"But—"

"Please, Harper. Let me cry this out, and then we can eat and talk shit. I just need to process what happened."

And then the line goes dead. I drop my phone into my lap and look at Jakob, whose brow is furrowed. "What happened?"

"Elli found Shea kissing her sister."

He makes a face, reaching for his phone. "No fucking way. Shea hates Victoria for how mean she is to Elli."

"That's what I thought," I say as he taps his phone.

He holds it to his ear and then makes a face. "Dude, what the fuck? No shit. Did you tell her that? No, she won't talk to Harper either. Go over there. Oh. Well, fuck." He looks over at me. "He's saying Victoria kissed him and he tried to get her off him, but she wouldn't move. He tried to tell Elli this, but she won't listen." Sounds about right. I really didn't think Shea would do that. I've seen the way he is with Elli; he loves her with everything inside him. "He said Victoria and Olivia talked him into going ring shopping together, and then Victoria kissed him after saying they should be together. When he pushed her away, Elli was there. He sounds fucked up. I believe him."

"I do too," I say, but I know Elli won't hear that right now. "Elli needs time. Victoria is awful to her, mentally abuses her to the point where Elli doesn't think she is good enough. She needs time to process, and hopefully she'll get her head out of her ass and realize the truth. Tell him to keep calling."

He tells his best friend that, and I watch as they talk. My heart aches for my best friend, and I don't know how something this awful can happen. I want to physically beat the shit out of Victoria. Lord knows she needs a good ass-whooping. The baby in my belly is keeping me from doing that. I need Elli to do it, to stand up for herself, but from the way she sounded, that's going to take a while. Man, I've always hated that sister of hers. She has always been awful to Elli, calling her fat, making fun of her, because she is jealous. Elli is the most amazing woman I have ever met, and hell, sometimes I'm even jealous of how put together she is.

When Jakob hangs up his phone, we share a look. "Well, that sucks."

I nod. "Yeah," I say as tears fill my eyes. "I can't ask Elli to stand beside me as I get married with all this going on."

Jakob holds my gaze. "Then we should wait." I fully expected him to say let's do this without them, but I must have forgotten Jakob is not like other men. "We can get married whenever. Because no matter what, you're my sunshine, my better half, and it's gonna happen."

I lean over as my tears start to fall. He wraps his arms around me, holding me close as his lips get lost in my hair. "We won't break up, will we?"

"Never," he promises. "You make life too easy for me to ever let you go. I hope I do the same."

"You do." I rub my hand along my face, catching my tears. "I can't believe this. They're supposed to get married and have babies."

"They will," he says, kissing my head. "This is just a roadblock they'll get through. I truly believe in them."

"I hope you're right," I say, my heart aching. I want to go to Elli's so bad, but I have to respect her wishes.

"I am," he whispers, kissing me once more. "And I think you should go to Elli's. I think she needs you."

I cuddle into him, squeezing him tight. "I think so too." I kiss his jaw, and he kisses my nose. "I love you."

"I love you."

And as I head out, I know I have it all.

The man, the home, and soon, the baby.

I just want the same for Elli and Shea.

NO, WE'RE GOING TO LIVE HAPPILY EVER AFTER

JAKOB

"I got into it really bad with Elli."

Harper's voice is clouded with emotion, and I hate it. I don't want her stressed, but she worries about Elli like she's her own. It's been two months since Shea and Elli broke up, and these last two months have been absolute hell. Elli is dead set that Shea cheated, while Shea is screaming his innocence. He has tried over and over again to get her to talk to him, but it hasn't worked. I thought Harper was reluctant, but she was easy peasy compared to Elli. The thing is, we believe him, and we hate that Elli is choosing to be unhappy rather than give him a chance to explain.

Harper having it out with Elli isn't a surprise. She's fed up. We all are. Shea and Elli are both hurting, and instead of fixing it, they're dying inside. It's more Elli than Shea, but it isn't like Shea is making good choices. Instead of fighting, he's drinking. Something that I don't tolerate. Since we both consider the two of them family, we're hurting too. We want to get married, but we refuse to do it without our best friends.

"What did she say?"

"I begged her to go to that event with us since Shea is going, but she won't. I told her she better get it together or we can't be friends."

"Harper, that's rough," I scold, but she doesn't care.

"She is choosing this. She still very much loves him. I'm hollering at her that we're engaged and I'm pregnant, and she wasn't even happy for me. I know she is hurting and she misses him, but again, she is choosing this misery and, in the process, being selfish."

"But in her defense, you didn't tell her right away—"

"Hush, you. She's being dumb. She needs a wake-up call." I don't know that I agree with the way Harper handled our news, but I know she won't cut Elli off. She loves her too much. I understand that Elli hasn't been there for Harper these last couple months, but she is hurting. Yes, she can fix it, but I don't think she sees it that way. "Did you talk to Shea?"

"I'm outside his place now."

"Don't let him say no."

"He'll go. I'm just checking on him at this point."

"Okay, call me back."

"Will do. Love you."

"Love you," she says, and I hang up.

I tuck my phone into my pocket and get out of the truck. When I look up at the house that Shea had bought for him and Elli, my stomach sinks. I tell Harper all the time that Shea and Elli will work it out, but if I'm honest, I'm not sure I believe it. There is some serious damage, and I worry that these two months have done nothing but put one hell of a wedge between them. After I walk up his drive, I don't knock before I enter. The house is empty. He didn't bring any furniture because he wants Elli to decorate.

Pathetic, I know, but I would be the same way.

"Shea?" I call out, and he comes stumbling out of the kitchen.

"Jakob? Knock much?"

I roll my eyes before looking at my watch. "It's not even noon."

He shrugs, visibly drunk. "It's five o'clock somewhere." He lowers himself into the beanbag he has, and everything inside me turns to anger.

"This is fucking ridiculous, Shea!" I yell, and he looks up at me.

"You can't talk to me about this. You're happy. You don't know what I am feeling."

I glare. "I do because I'm your best friend, you idiot," I say, reaching for the cup he is drinking from and throwing it in the trash. "You aren't helping the situation, and you've given up."

He shrugs, leaning his head back. "Who cares? She won't take me back."

"Because you gave up!" I yell, crouching down so I'm at his level. "I never gave up with Harper. I fought for her, I wanted her, and look at us. We're happy."

"Yeah, but you don't have her sisters trying to break you guys up. The world is against us."

"Then go against the world!" I demand, glaring at him. "This isn't you."

He shrugs, and I can see the defeat in his whole body. "Jakob, I don't know how to get her back."

"Fight for her. Make her realize that you are it."

"How?"

"Make her see that you still love her. Don't stop until you get her."

He shakes his head. "It won't work."

"Not when you have that way of thinking." It kills me to see him like this. He's been sucking on the ice. And off the ice, he's a mess. "The first thing to do is stop drinking. It isn't going to help you."

"It numbs everything."

I ignore that. "And stop with the females. They won't replace her."

"I haven't even slept with anyone."

"You're trying to. To stop hurting." I hate this. "I believe in you two. You need to believe, too."

Tears cloud his blue eyes. "I do, but I don't think she does."

"Then show her what to believe in."

He sits there for a second and then nods. "Okay."

"Okay," I say slowly. "Now, get a shower and get ready for tonight."

He runs his hands down his face. "Yeah, I'll be there. You and Harper going to be there?"

"Yeah," I say, standing up. "I asked her to marry me."

He looks up at me. "Yeah?"

"Yeah, and she said yes."

"That's wonderful, man," he says, but like Harper suspected, he doesn't care any more than Elli because of their own pain.

"She's pregnant, too."

His shoulders fall. "Well, don't you have it all."

"I do," I say, setting him with a look. "And you could too. You just can't give up."

Because if he does, he'll lose everything.

When you have it all, you want the same for the people you love.

I hold Harper's hand as we wait for the ultrasound technician.

"I still can't believe he showed up with someone."

I cringe, unable to look Harper in the eye. That's my fault. I should have told Shea we were trying to get Elli to come to the benefit; I just never thought he'd show up with a date. I swallow hard as I nod. "I can't believe it either."

"Elli is heartbroken."

The guilt is eating me alive. Why didn't I tell him? "I can imagine."

"She's going by Grace's today. She's giving Ryan all of Shea's memorabilia. I think she might be done. I tried to talk her out of it, but it didn't work."

Fantastic. "I'm hoping Shea can figure something out."

"Me too," she says softly, and then the technician comes in.

"Mrs. and Mr. Titov?" We both nod, and I grin over at her. We aren't married yet, but Harper doesn't correct anyone. I don't either. "Great, let's see what we've got in here. We're finding out the sex, right?"

"Yes, we need to know so we can paint," Harper gushes, and I kiss the back of her hand, leaning on her hip bone. As much as I'm worried about Shea and Elli, watching my woman grow my child takes precedence over everything else. The Assassins are making one hell of a run to the play-offs, and I should be stoked, proud of us, but seeing this child grow is what fills me with the most pride. Harper glances at me, and when she cups my face, I beam over at her. This woman completes me.

We both watch as the tech puts some goop on Harper's belly before moving the probe along it. When my child comes on the screen, everything inside me freezes. My jaw drops, and my heart damn near explodes in my chest. "That's it?"

The tech grins and then points at the screen. "That's her. Y'all's daughter."

Within seconds, an unbelievably protective feeling comes over me. Harper whips her gaze to mine, and our eyes lock in a loving and overpowering way. Tears gather in her eyes, and when they start to fall, I realize that I'm about to love two perfect females for the rest of my life. Really, no one can be that lucky, can they?

But then I look back at the screen, see my future, and I know it's true.

WOULD HE BE THERE FOR YOU?

HARPER

I will never get over how gorgeous my daughter is. I might be biased, but I happen to think she is the most amazing and perfect human on this planet. I will also never forget the day I found out we were having a girl. I remember lying there, seeing my whole world come together as Jakob looked at me like I had given him the best gift ever. What he didn't know was he had given me the same.

His love.

His forever.

Two kids later, our life is pretty great.

Has it been easy? Hell no. But we fought for each other. For our family. And I wouldn't trade our hard days for anything. They shaped us into two great people who are raising two fantastic kids. This is one of those bad days, but I truly believe Ally will do what is right. And if she doesn't, I'm blaming it all on Jakob.

He has spoiled us all.

"But Uncle Shea and Aunt Elli are together." Ally looks

confused as she glances between the two of us. "Like, super-together."

I scoff. "Well, it didn't look good for the home team."

Jakob laughs.

"He showed up to that benefit with a girl, and it broke Aunt Elli's heart. All over again."

"We all know the story, though, of how he broke the glass to get her attention, and then she sang for him. I mean, we've all watched the tape," Ally says, a perplexed look still on her face. "But I never knew they had broken up."

Jakob nods. "Yeah. No one really knows that they were broken for a long time before all that happened. We all forget the bad because the good is so damn good."

Ally just blinks. "It is insane that y'all only told us the good."

"Because why would we tell you the bad, sweetheart?" I ask, holding her sweet gaze. "Maybe that's where we messed up. All of you think things just work out, but the truth is, you have to work at this."

"It isn't easy," Jakob says. "Mom had to stay beside me all the times we thought my career was over. I was not nice and I drove her crazy, but she loved me."

"When I lost all those babies between you and Journey, and then with Jamie," I say, my voice breaking at the thought of our stillborn baby. Man, it was a rough time, but Jakob was there with me. Always there. "I wanted to give up, but Daddy wouldn't let me. He loved me." Our eyes lock, and the last twenty some odd years fly by me. "When he got hurt that second time and got hooked on those pain meds, I thought I had lost the man I loved. But still, I never left his side. I helped him get back to my man."

Jakob's eyes widen. We don't speak of that year. It was a rough time, and I saw my marriage ending just like his career had. But I think I'm too stubborn to have let that happen. I married this man for a reason, and that's because he never gave up on me. I couldn't do that to him. Not with how much I loved him. While I don't know that Ally needs to know the details, I need her to realize that relationships aren't easy. That unless Taco is going to fight for her like she is trying to fight for him, it won't work. I already know he won't. Look at what he is wanting her to do. That's not looking out for her best interests, and I hope hearing this will make her realize that.

Jakob looks down at where he is holding my hand and squeezes. "And I wouldn't have made it if your mom hadn't loved me through it."

Ally looks at her dad. "We all loved you through that."

He nods, wrapping his arm around her neck and kissing her head. "Exactly. And we made it because we made sure not to give up on each other."

She looks up at him, and soon, my eyes are filling with tears. I love how much he loves her. How much he loves us all. "I just want what y'all have."

He kisses her head once more. "And we want the same for you. But, *svet*…"

Svet means light, and it's something he has called her since she was born.

Jakob holds her tightly and says, "You have it all right now, and you're working so hard for everything. Why do you want to give it up to go with this boy, losing all that you've worked for just to be with someone who won't encourage you to pursue your dreams?"

I mean, I asked the same question and she didn't listen to me, but I see her listening to her father. She leans her head into him and looks up at me. "I love Taco."

Jakob shrugs as he hugs her. "I happen to be partial to Mexican pizzas now, but there was—"

"Dad," she says dryly, and I can't help but snicker.

He grins, holding her face. "You're only twenty-two, *svet*, so young. Even at twenty-nine, your mom didn't know I was it. Hell, I didn't fall in love until I was almost thirty."

I see the fight in her eyes, and I hold up my hands. "I know it can happen sooner, I know Shelli and Aiden are getting married, and blah, blah, blah. But honey, Shelli lived a lot before she settled down. Aiden, the same. We just want you to grow. To figure yourself out."

"That's all we want," Jakob agrees. "So, you need to ask yourself—would he be there for you?"

Thank you, Jakob. I want to squash his face and kiss the shit out of him as I watch the wheels turn in Ally's head. I squeeze her knee, and she looks up at me. "We are so proud of you. You are such an amazing human, Allison, and we love you more than all the words in the world. We want what's best for you, and we truly believe finishing school is what is best. After that, you can decide if you want to start a life with Taco."

She shakes her head, and my stomach drops. "He won't want to do long-distance."

"Then he isn't the one. Your volleyball career and your studies are very important. Don't you think so?"

She looks away and then nods slowly. "Yeah, but I love him."

I hate this part of her. I love that she loves, but it makes her so irrational.

"But is it love for him to ask this of you?" Jakob asks, and she looks up at him. "I get it. Love is an addiction, especially when it comes to your mother."

Wow, talk about hitting you in the feels. Even after over twenty years, this man leaves me breathless.

"I was ready to give it all up for her, but she wouldn't let me. She wanted to grow together, and I think we did a damn good job of it."

I nod. "We did."

He winks, and my heart soars. This man is my life.

Ally clears her throat. "If y'all are gonna make eyes at each other, can you go into another room? I need to think."

Jakob laughs as I smile. He drops a kiss on her head and then gets up. "We'll always be here for you."

I cup her face, brushing my thumb along her cherubic cheeks. "And we'll always love you. No matter what."

Ally leans into my hand and smiles sweetly. "I love you both."

My heart can't take it, and I need to get out of there. As I shut her door behind me, Jakob wraps his arms around me, kissing me hard on the lips. I squeeze my arms around his neck, and when he pulls back, I smile. "She's gonna make the right decision."

My heart skips a beat. "I hope you're right."

He grins. "I was right about us."

I lean my head into his nose. He was and I'm thankful he was, but I just pray he's right about this.

Because I want nothing more than for my daughter to live the life she deserves.

With a man who loves her as much as her daddy loves me.

IT'S YOURS. YOU JUST GOTTA TAKE IT.

JAKOB

When I took the job as special teams coach, I didn't realize I would love it as much as I do. I always loved special teams; I was one badass power play scorer. But I never thought this was what I would do when my hockey playing career ended. I thought I'd sit at home and be a stay-at-home dad, but I realized very quickly, I get bored. So, Elli offered me this job, and I jumped at the chance. Not only do I get to coach, but I get a nifty office. I never saw myself as an office guy, but I have to admit, I love it.

On my desk is a picture of Harper and me on our wedding day. We didn't have a full-on wedding; we went down to the courthouse with Shea and Elli and our families when Harper was seven months pregnant. She's exquisite, glowing and perfect in her flowy purple dress. I'll never forget that day. It was one for the highlight reels. There are also pictures of us with the kids when they were born, but the picture that really has me in my feelings is the one of Ally the day she graduated high school. Harper and I are looking at her with such pride in our eyes, and it kills me to think she might throw it all away. I don't think she will, but she is really in love with this Taco fuck.

I look back at the picture of Harper and me. I wasn't kidding when I said love is an addiction when it comes to her. Nothing comes close to the way she makes me feel. I yearn for it, and I understand where Ally is coming from. She's a romantic, just like me. I just hope she realizes this guy won't love her the way she needs to be loved. Some would have said the same about Harper when I was chasing her, but I always knew she was the one. I don't think Ally genuinely believes Taco is for her.

A knock at the door pulls my attention, and a grin comes over my face. "Posey, I see you got my message."

Posey Adler, Shea and Elli's second daughter, smiles timidly at me. While everyone is usually so blown away by their eldest daughter, Shelli, Posey has always been my favorite. She's a quiet but spunky little thing and smart as a whip when it comes to hockey. She looks just like her mom, auburn hair and curvy. Some say she isn't as pretty as Shelli, but I disagree. She reminds me a lot of Elli. A timeless beauty.

"Did you see the plays I had the boys running?"

She grins as she sits down. "I saw Boon mess it all up."

I shrug, a little guilty. "Yeah. I don't think I explained it right."

"Probably not. I mean, it is my play."

I nod as I tap my knuckles to my desk. "You got a job yet?"

She makes a face. She just graduated from Bellevue—a year early, of course, given her drive—with a degree in Information Technology. She once told me she didn't see herself actually going into the field, but there isn't a college degree for coaching in the NHL. She played in college and could have gone all the way, but she doesn't love playing as much as she loves making plays. She's a smart cookie. "No. Still figuring things out. I've had offers, but I don't know."

Just what I want to hear. When I say this girl is hockey smart, I'm not kidding. It's like all the knowledge from Shea and Elli morphed into one and made Posey. Shelli and the boys are smart, but Posey is able to read things no one else can. I wished she had played professionally for the WNHL, but it wasn't her passion. She wanted to be on the play-making side of things, and after discussing it with her mom for hours on end, I believe I have her dream job.

"Listen, the reason I asked you here is because I want you to be my assistant coach for special teams."

Her face is like stone, her blue eyes blazing as she holds my gaze. "Really?"

"Really. I talked to your mom and sister, and they agree. We need you."

She licks her lips as she looks down at her hands. "So, Shelli actually said she wanted me?"

"She was insistent," I confirm.

Posey looks surprised as she glances at her nails, making a disgruntled noise. I'm not sure why, but before I can ask that, she says, "But what about the coach you have now?"

"He's out. His plays aren't readable or teachable, and he's not giving us what we need. We think you could be what we need."

Her eyes bore into mine. "I don't know."

Not what I was expecting. I raise my brow. "You don't know?"

She looks up then. "I think I might go to Colorado for a bit."

"Colorado? What's there?"

Her expression changes, and her face fills with color. Then I realize it's not what, but who.

"You're going after Maxim?"

She shrugs, and I let my head hang. Maxim was the billet boy who lived with Shea's family for four years until he was finally called up to the farm team for the Avalanche.

"I still can't believe Daddy shipped him off. And I don't know… I feel like things can happen."

I make a face. What is up with girls these days? These boys don't care about them. We all know about her crush on Maxim, but he was too busy fucking Lucas Brooks's daughter. It was the main reason Shea shipped him off; he was saving Posey from making a fool of herself. The guy had no feelings for her whatsoever. He only saw her as a friend. I bet Shea never saw this Colorado trip coming.

"Do your parents know?"

She shakes her head. "No."

"You going to tell them?"

She smiles. "When I get there."

"Jesus," I groan, shaking my head.

"Please don't tell them."

I think about it for a second. The thing is, I know she'll be back. "I will keep your secret as long as—if you do come back—you'll take the job."

She swallows hard. "I don't know that I will be back. I love him."

If I hear one more child tell me she loves some shit dude, I'm going to scream. "Just say you will if you do."

She doesn't even hesitate. "I will."

"Great," I say with a smile. "Now, come give your uncle a hug, and may the force be with you."

She laughs as we get up and embrace. I kiss her temple and hug her tightly. "Don't settle for anything less than perfection, you hear me?"

"I do."

"And the job is yours. You just gotta take it."

She nods, holding me tightly. "I hear you."

Man, I hope she does.

As we part, another knock comes to my door. I look up to see Ally grinning. "Posey!"

Posey lets me go, and the girls embrace tightly. "You didn't call me when you got back in town!"

Posey shakes her head. "Dude, I made such a fool of myself at Amelia's wedding," she says, covering her face. "Wanna go to dinner?"

"Heck yeah. Let me talk to my dad, and I'll meet you at Brooks House."

Posey hugs her once more. "Cool. We have a lot to talk about."

"We sure do," Ally says as Posey waves to me.

"Bye, Jakob."

"Bye, honey. Be careful."

She grins back at me and waves once more. I want to call Shea right then and tell him, but I know it won't work out for her. She'll be back. Plus, we all know Shea will lose his ever-loving mind. He doesn't even believe his kids are sexually active. He lives in some kind of fantasyland. I know, and while I hate it, it's a part of life. Lord knows Harper and I do it all the time. Even with my shit arm, I'm still able to hold her ass up and get it.

Ally closes the door and then sits down in one of the chairs in front of my desk.

"What brings you by?" I ask as I sit on my desk. "Didn't you have practice?"

"It ended an hour ago, Daddy," she says with a roll of her eyes. She acts like I can keep up with her life; she's always busy. "I just had coffee with Taco."

I find that I'm holding my breath. "Coffee? I thought you guys would have gone for tacos."

Her eyes darken. "Daddy."

"Sorry. How did it go?"

"Yeah, I told him I wasn't going with him," she says slowly, not looking at me. "He broke up with me."

Fucker. I stand up, taking her hand and bringing her out of the chair and into my chest. "Oh, *svet*, I'm sorry."

She holds me tightly, her tears soaking my dress shirt. "I couldn't believe it. He didn't even pause or anything. He just said, 'Fine. We're done, then.'"

Motherfucker. "I'm sorry."

"Y'all were right."

"It happens sometimes," I joke, kissing her forehead. "But at least you know now."

"Yeah, before I threw it all away and chased after him."

"This is true," I say, kissing her once more. "You know you're going to be just fine."

"I know," she says, holding me. "But it sucks. I just want my version of Jakob Titov."

I grin against her forehead. "Don't worry. You'll find him."

When Ally leaves to meet Posey, I sit back in my chair and exhale heavily. I reach for the phone and dial Harper's number. She answers right away, and her voice sends me to the clouds. I close my eyes as I sigh. "Hey, *kiska*."

"Hey, when are you coming home? I need you to stop for bread. We're having French toast for dinner."

I grin. "That sounds fantastic. I'll be leaving in a bit. I wanted to call you, though."

"You okay?"

"Yeah, I just love you."

I can hear the grin in her voice. "I love you, baby."

When she tells me those words, it's always like I'm hearing them for the first time. "Ally came to see me."

"Oh? I thought she went out with Posey."

"She did, but she came to see me first."

"What for?"

"Taco broke up with her when she told him she wouldn't go with him."

"That motherfucker!" she yells. "I knew it! Didn't I tell her that?"

"We both did, and she agreed we were right," I say as I lean back. "She's staying home, though."

"Oh, Jakob," she cries. Maybe I should have waited until I got home. I could have held her, but I wanted to tell her right away. "I was so worried."

"Me too," I agree as I close my eyes. "Great job, team."

She laughs. "Well, you are the best teammate."

"Right back atcha."

"Really, it was smart to tell her everything."

"I thought so," I say softly. "But I think it was a team effort."

"It always is." She lets out a long sigh. "She's gonna find someone so good for her."

"She wants her 'Jakob Titov.'"

She pokes fun at me. "Good luck. Nothing but fuckboys out there."

I grin. "She'll find him."

"I did."

I smile.

"I love you so much, Jakob. Seriously. You're the best father and husband ever."

I grin as I sit up. "Didn't I promise you a damn good life?"

"You did."

"And I won't ever break that promise."

"I know, which only makes me love you even more."

If only she knew how much I fall for her over and over again. "And you thought I was only a one-time thing."

She scoffs. "I was completely wrong. I'm just glad you never gave up."

I grin because life hasn't been easy, but she makes it pretty damn great.

"And I never will."

That's an easy promise to keep when it comes to her.

THE END

NASHVILLE ASSASSINS

Breaking Away

Laces and Lace

A Very Merry Hockey Holiday

Wanting to Forget

Overtime

Rushing the Goal

Puck, Sticks, and Diapers

Face-off at the Altar

Delayed Call

Twenty-Two

In the Crease

One Timer

Nashville Assassins: Next Generation

Dump & Chase

Power Play

Bellevue Bullies Series

Boarded by Love

Clipped by Love

Hooked by Love

End Game

IceCats Series

Juicy Rebound

Wild Tendy

Taking Risks

Whiskey Prince

Becoming the Whiskey Princess

Whiskey Rebellion

Patchwork Series

(Paranormal)

Pieces

Broken Pieces

Spring Grove Novels

(Small-town romances)

Not the One

Small-Town Sweetheart

Nobody's Sweetheart (Coming SOON!)

Standalones

Let it be Me

Two-Man Advantage

Misadventures

(Standalones)

Misadventures with a Rookie

Misadventures of a Manny

Assassins Series

Taking Shots

Trying to Score

Empty Net

Falling for the Backup

Blue Lines

ACKNOWLEDGMENTS

As always, first, I want to thank YOU.

You are the reason I keep writing and why I am living my best life. You mean so much to me, and I love you. Thank you.

Second, I want to thank Lisa. She's been urging me to write this book FOREVER. She was right; it is awesome. She has stood beside me through thick and thin. I love you, Holletta. Thank you.

I want to thank my husband, my babies, my dogs, and my Bobbie. I am so blessed in the life department, and I stoked for my future.

I want to thank my amazing betas without whom this book wouldn't be what it is. These women make me a better writer and love me even when I don't love myself. Thank you, Heather, Jessica, Laurie, Franci, Susie, Althea, and Nikki.

I hope you enjoyed One Timer and are excited for Power Play. I know I am! Please remember that a review is like a HUGE hug. I love them. Thank you again.

Love,
Toni

ABOUT TONI ALEO

My name is Toni Aleo, and I'm a #PredHead, #sherrio,
#potterhead, and part of the #familybusiness!
I am also a wife to my amazing husband, mother of a gamer
and a gymnast, and also a fur momma to Gaston el Papillion
& Winnie Pooh.
While my beautiful and amazing Shea Weber has been traded
from my Predators, I'm still a huge fan. But when I'm not
cheering for him, I'm hollering for the whole Nashville
Predators since I'll never give my heart to one player again.
When I'm not in the gym getting swole, I'm usually writing,
trying to make my dreams a reality, or being a taxi for my
kids.
I'm obsessed with Harry Potter, Supernatural, Disney, and
anything that sparkles! I'm pretty sure I was Belle in a past

life, and if I could be on any show, it would be Supernatural so I could hunt with Sam and Dean.
Also, I did mention I love hockey, right?

Also make sure to join the mailing list for up to date news from Toni Aleo:
JOIN NOW!

www.tonialeo.com
toni@tonialeo.com

Made in the USA
Lexington, KY
28 November 2019

57702071R00083